WHISPERED PROMISES OF LOVE

MG SINGH

Dedicated to my mother Swarn Kaur-fond remembrances ever

Contents

Foreword

Preface

The book is a collection of previously published short stories. The stories have an erotic touch and make interesting reading. They are set in the subcontinent and draw heavily on the authors' experience. This book can be part of a traveler's baggage or a bedtime read. Many of the stories have a supernatural aura that adds to the flavor.

Whispering Tales of Love

WHISPERED PROMISES OF LOVE
BY
MG SINGH

YAMINI

I am going to tell you the story of Yamini. What an exotic name what does it mean? Yamini was the daughter of Daksha Prajapati, and was won the one of the wives of Kasaypa. Many will be wondering who was Daksha Prajapat? Well friends, Daksha is one of the Prajapati, who is the agent of creation as well as the divine king also known as king Rishi. This beautiful girl in Hindu mythology was the daughter of this king. Yamini also means night, and that means twilight and darkness with twinkling stars and the moon shining in the sky. Who was Kasaypa? he is the Vedic sage of Hinduism and one of the seven ancient sages of the Rig Veda.

I have spent a few moments giving you details of this name because this is a secret name and I happened to have come across this name and the girl in a meeting which is perhaps ordained by God.

The story begins when I drove down into the hills. It was a route which was well known to me and one which I had travelled almost every day for close to a decade. I was familiar with the road, but frankly, I was not aware that there was the temple hidden by a clump of trees which I discovered by accident, despite having driven the road for almost a decade. The temple was not very big. That was the reason it remained hidden from my vision.

It was raining heavily, and the visibility has been reduced to zero and the wipers of the car were running at full speed and yet I couldn't see a thing. Visibility beyond the windscreen was nil. With this situation, I thought it best to stop for some time. I pulled up in front of a clump of trees. I had been seeing this clump for many years. It was a thick clump, and I was sure to get protection from the rain here. I got down from his car and then realized that this was not perhaps the best place to save myself. It could be dangerous because lightning was flashing across the sky, and I had read of cases of people taking shelter under a tree being hit by lightning and so I was alert and started looking around for a better place to save myself. The rain continued to beat on the earth, taking all decisions out of my hand.

I looked around and despite the poor visibility and the heavy rain falling, I could make out that just behind the clump of trees was a temple. I decided the blessed place could be a refuge for me come from the elements of nature. I estimated the distance to be about 10 m and I am moved towards the temple. I negotiated the thick undergrowth and low and behold, I was standing before the temple. The rain had now picked up and it had turned into a thunderstorm; lightning was flashing across the sky and thunder boomed again and again. I thought it best to spend time in the temple till the storm abated. I reached the temple and saw that it was not large, yet I sensed that it was hundreds of years old. It was in a delipidated condition, but I was safe in the foyer of the temple. I had a look inside the sanctum sanatorium and could see the image of Lord Shiva and I realized that this was the temple dedicated to the creator, and the destroyer in Hinduism.

I was wondering what would happen next. I was surprised when a heard a cough of a girl. I looked around but couldn't see anybody. This was because of an optical illusion as the outside was relatively bright and inside dark. I went inside the temple; it was a spontaneous decision and without thinking I entered the temple. My eyes took a moment to adjust to the darkness inside. I could make out the statue of Lord Shiva looking down on me and then I was in for a shock for standing next to the godly figure was a beautiful girl and I was even more shocked to realize that she was the same girl who had met me in the Publishers office way back in Chennai. I recognized the beautiful girl who was now wearing a lovely sari tied low down that accentuated her slim waist.

"Yamini," I asked," what the hell are you doing here?"

She did not reply immediately, but after a moment said," I don't know"

"But I had met you in Egmore"

"I really don't know. The last, I remember is that I was in Egmore in my office and from there I had gone with you to my apartment and now I find myself here."

"It is not possible" I said," such thing happens only in fantasy or in mythology."

"I agree, but we are both of us going through this experience."

I thought for a moment then replied," I can't see anything, but I remember that Arasu your boss was sitting on the table and facing me, and you had entered with the files, and I must say I liked you very much but how come you're here"

"I do not know," she replied." but I understand you are a follower of Lord Krishna, and his color is blue, and it is possible, he is the one who has sent me here."

"It's not possible."

"You may be wrong"

I thought the girl is making a fool of me and I said," this is a lot of bullshit. I am pretty sure you came by Air India and then you took a taxi or something and came here to this God forsaken temple."

She was silent for a moment and then I asked," what next? Do you really believe what you told me that you didn't know anything, and you just materialized at this place?"

"I don't know what to say"?

I was now confused and wondering whether what was happening was a dream or reality. I looked at the sky. It had turned blue and that was a bit of a surprise because the thunder is gone, and it was all so beautiful.

"Listen, Yamini, "I said," don't make a fool of me. I remember we sat in your editor's office, and we discussed my book and suddenly now you appear before me. I'm sure you came here from Chennai, and you must have known about my movements. Frankly I don't believe whatever you are talking."

Yamini paused for a moment and then said," sir I am here and as surprised as you I had gone to sleep and then I got up and I found myself here in the foyer of the temple"

All I could say was," bullshit"

The sky, which had cleared up, once again darkened and clouds began to cover the sky, and thunder crashed across the heavens, and once more, the heavy downpour commenced. Then an electrifying moment took place; lightning crashed and hit a tree in the compound of the temple, just about 30 feet away from where we were standing. There was a crackling sound as the tree caught fire and the resultant smoke and sound frightened Yamini who rushed to me, and I held in my arms and that is the time I realized what a bundle she was, so warm and alive.

"Come closer," I whispered.

I pulled the pulsating girl towards me, and as I enveloped her, I could hear the beating of her heart as it was thumping loudly. Something strange happened next which I cannot explain because I began to kiss Yamini and she reciprocated and the back of my mind, I was wondering what the hell is going on but the crashing all around and holding the girl close to me dulled my thinking capability. I had no time to think, but then Yamini probably realized what was happening and she pushed me away and began to run away, but she slipped and fell on the grass outside and now the rain was beating on her. She tried to cover her face with her arms to escape the rain pouring on her.

I quickly remove my shirt with the intention of covering her and went over, but she looks so lovely and with the rain beating on her with the blouse and saree clinging to her body, bringing out her beauty in relief and I am mesmerized. I am overwhelmed by the sight, and I hover over her and begin to kiss her. I can't stop and kiss her again and again. The rain is falling all around, and it begins to beat on my back, but I don't mind. I am overtaken by desire, and unbutton her blouse and push up her bra, baring her nipples to my sight. I began to suckle them like a child, and after a moment go over to her lips covering her completely, so that rain is beating on my back. One thing leads to another, and now I am conscious, I have moved to the altar of her beauty and find my face hidden there with the rain beating down. This is the decisive moment, and a little later I possess her. The storm is now getting violent and again, lightning hits a stump a hundred yards away. This was the moment and Yamini gave a small yelp like a puppy and I knew that her state had changed from girl to woman.

Much later, I got up and carried her inside the temple which was well protected from the rain and continued kissing her, and then I began to feel anger and close my eyes and I do not know what happened because I fell asleep.

You all know the story of the Rip Van Winkle the man who went to sleep and slept for 20 years. It is something similar only I didn't sleep for 20 years but I got up very shortly after a nap and looked around, but Yamini had vanished, and I was wondering what happened and where she had gone? perhaps I thought she had gone back to Chennai.

I shouted her name, but there was no response. The rain continued and after waiting for almost an hour the rain stopped and I went to my SUV and sat in the seat and wondered what happened. I really had no explanation at all.

I put my SUV into gear and the vehicle moves forward, but at the same time I felt lighthearted, and I wondered why. I was wondering how the girl from Chennai had materialized in the temple in front of me and then vanished. I left the temple and continued along the slow winding road back home. I went to my apartment and from there I immediately dialed the Chennai number of my Publisher. He came online and I asked him, "listen pal, where is Yamini?"

"Very much here"

"Are you sure?"

"Absolutely"

I switched off the mobile and at the same time decided that I am go down to Chennai to investigate what had happened but as I was just getting into bed, I had a call from my director, and he told me that I had to come to America to discuss the layoffs of few people as the Covid epidemic had got out of hand.

I never made it to Chennai and after two months, I returned to India. As I entered, my mobile rang and I switched it on, and I was absolutely thrilled that it was Yamini.

"Is that you?" I asked

"Yes," she replied, "it's me."

"From where you are talking?"

"I am talking from an Ashram in Sikkim, where I've come down for rest and recuperation"

"What are you doing there, rest and recuperation is a bit silly."

"Are you surprised?"

She continued, "I needed rest as you remember that after you left you picked me up and dropped me to my apartment and I invited you for a cup of coffee and then that beautiful moment took place between us. You can't forget it."

"But we met at the temple."

"Don't talk nonsense we never met in any temple. We were in my house in my room."

"Can you explain?" I asked

There was no reply and the click told me she had dropped the line.

I realized that I had been part of a great mystery which had been created by the supernatural. Perhaps what happened was a hallucination but what had happened in Yamini apartment was the absolute truth. I just sat and stared at the hills outside my window.

YAMINI

I am going to tell you the story of Yamini. What an exotic name what does it mean? Yamini was the daughter of Daksha Prajapati, and was won the one of the wives of Kasaypa. Many will be wondering who was Daksha Prajapat? Well friends, Daksha is one of the Prajapati, who is the agent of creation as well as the divine king also known as king Rishi. This beautiful girl in Hindu mythology was the daughter of this king. Yamini also means night, and that means twilight and darkness with twinkling stars and the moon shining in the sky. Who was Kasaypa? he is the Vedic sage of Hinduism and one of the seven ancient sages of the Rig Veda.

I have spent a few moments giving you details of this name because this is a secret name and I happened to have come across this name and the girl in a meeting which is perhaps ordained by God.

The story begins when I drove down into the hills. It was a route which was well known to me and one which I had travelled almost every day for close to a decade. I was familiar with the road, but frankly, I was not aware that there was the temple hidden by a clump of trees which I discovered by accident, despite having driven the road for almost a decade. The temple was not very big. That was the reason it remained hidden from my vision.

It was raining heavily, and the visibility has been reduced to zero and the wipers of the car were running at full speed and yet I couldn't see a thing. Visibility beyond the windscreen was nil. With this situation, I thought it best to stop for some time. I pulled up in front of a clump of trees. I had been seeing this clump for many years. It was a thick clump, and I was sure to get protection from the rain here. I got down from his car and then realized that this was not perhaps the best place to save myself. It could be dangerous because lightning was flashing across the sky, and I had read of cases of people taking shelter under a tree being hit by lightning and so I was alert and started looking around for a better place to save myself. The rain continued to beat on the earth, taking all decisions out of my hand.

I looked around and despite the poor visibility and the heavy rain falling, I could make out that just behind the clump of trees was a temple. I decided the blessed place could be a refuge for me come from the elements of nature. I estimated the distance to be about 10 m and I am moved towards the temple. I negotiated the thick undergrowth and low and behold, I was standing before the temple. The rain had now picked up and it had turned into a thunderstorm; lightning was flashing across the sky and thunder boomed again and again. I thought it best to spend time in the temple till the storm abated. I reached the temple and saw that it was not large, yet I sensed that it was hundreds of years old. It was in a delipidated condition, but I was safe in the foyer of the temple. I had a look inside the sanctum sanatorium and could see the image of Lord Shiva and I realized that this was the temple dedicated to the creator, and the destroyer in Hinduism.

I was wondering what would happen next. I was surprised when a heard a cough of a girl. I looked around but couldn't see anybody. This was because of an optical illusion as the outside was relatively bright and inside dark. I went inside the temple; it was a spontaneous decision and without thinking I entered the temple. My eyes took a moment to adjust to the darkness inside. I could make out the statue of Lord Shiva looking down on me and then I was in for a shock for standing next to the godly figure was a beautiful girl and I was even more shocked to realize that she was the same girl who had met me in the Publishers office way back in Chennai. I recognized the beautiful girl who was now wearing a lovely sari tied low down that accentuated her slim waist.

"Yamini," I asked," what the hell are you doing here?"

She did not reply immediately, but after a moment said," I don't know"

"But I had met you in Egmore"

"I really don't know. The last, I remember is that I was in Egmore in my office and from there I had gone with you to my apartment and now I find myself here."

"It is not possible" I said," such thing happens only in fantasy or in mythology."

"I agree, but we are both of us going through this experience."

I thought for a moment then replied," I can't see anything, but I remember that Arasu your boss was sitting on the table and facing me, and you had entered with the files, and I must say I liked you very much but how come you're here"

"I do not know," she replied." but I understand you are a follower of Lord Krishna, and his color is blue, and it is possible, he is the one who has sent me here."

"It's not possible."

"You may be wrong"

I thought the girl is making a fool of me and I said," this is a lot of bullshit. I am pretty sure you came by Air India and then you took a taxi or something and came here to this God forsaken temple."

She was silent for a moment and then I asked," what next? Do you really believe what you told me that you didn't know anything, and you just materialized at this place?"

"I don't know what to say"?

I was now confused and wondering whether what was happening was a dream or reality. I looked at the sky. It had turned blue and that was a bit of a surprise because the thunder is gone, and it was all so beautiful.

"Listen, Yamini, "I said," don't make a fool of me. I remember we sat in your editor's office, and we discussed my book and suddenly now you appear before me. I'm sure you came here from Chennai, and you must have known about my movements. Frankly I don't believe whatever you are talking."

Yamini paused for a moment and then said," sir I am here and as surprised as you I had gone to sleep and then I got up and I found myself here in the foyer of the temple"

All I could say was," bullshit"

The sky, which had cleared up, once again darkened and clouds began to cover the sky, and thunder crashed across the heavens, and once more, the heavy downpour commenced. Then an electrifying moment took place; lightning crashed and hit a tree in the compound of the temple, just about 30 feet away from where we were standing. There was a crackling sound as the tree caught fire and the resultant smoke and sound frightened Yamini who rushed to me, and I held in my arms and that is the time I realized what a bundle she was, so warm and alive.

"Come closer," I whispered.

I pulled the pulsating girl towards me, and as I enveloped her, I could hear the beating of her heart as it was thumping loudly. Something strange happened next which I cannot explain because I began to kiss Yamini and she reciprocated and the back of my mind, I was wondering what the hell is going on but the crashing all around and holding the girl close to me dulled my thinking capability. I had no time to think, but then Yamini probably realized what was happening and she pushed me away and began to run away, but she slipped and fell on the grass outside and now the rain was beating on her. She tried to cover her face with her arms to escape the rain pouring on her.

I quickly remove my shirt with the intention of covering her and went over, but she looks so lovely and with the rain beating on her with the blouse and saree clinging to her body, bringing out her beauty in relief and I am mesmerized. I am overwhelmed by the sight, and I hover over her and begin to kiss her. I can't stop and kiss her again and again. The rain is falling all around, and it begins to beat on my back, but I don't mind. I am overtaken by desire, and unbutton her blouse and push up her bra, baring her nipples to my sight. I began to suckle them like a child, and after a moment go over to her lips covering her completely, so that rain is beating on my back. One thing leads to another, and now I am conscious, I have moved to the altar of her beauty and find my face hidden there with the rain beating down. This is the decisive moment, and a little later I possess her. The storm is now getting violent and again, lightning hits a stump a hundred yards away. This was the moment and Yamini gave a small yelp like a puppy and I knew that her state had changed from girl to woman.

Much later, I got up and carried her inside the temple which was well protected from the rain and continued kissing her, and then I began to feel anger and close my eyes and I do not know what happened because I fell asleep.

You all know the story of the Rip Van Winkle the man who went to sleep and slept for 20 years. It is something similar only I didn't sleep for 20 years but I got up very shortly after a nap and looked around, but Yamini had vanished, and I was wondering what happened and where she had gone? perhaps I thought she had gone back to Chennai.

I shouted her name, but there was no response. The rain continued and after waiting for almost an hour the rain stopped and I went to my SUV and sat in the seat and wondered what happened. I really had no explanation at all.

I put my SUV into gear and the vehicle moves forward, but at the same time I felt lighthearted, and I wondered why. I was wondering how the girl from Chennai had materialized in the temple in front of me and then vanished. I left the temple and continued along the slow winding road back home. I went to my apartment and from there I immediately dialed the Chennai number of my Publisher. He came online and I asked him, "listen pal, where is Yamini?"

"Very much here"

"Are you sure?"

"Absolutely"

I switched off the mobile and at the same time decided that I am go down to Chennai to investigate what had happened but as I was just getting into bed, I had a call from my director, and he told me that I had to come to America to discuss the layoffs of few people as the Covid epidemic had got out of hand.

I never made it to Chennai and after two months, I returned to India. As I entered, my mobile rang and I switched it on, and I was absolutely thrilled that it was Yamini.

"Is that you?" I asked

"Yes," she replied, "it's me."

"From where you are talking?"

"I am talking from an Ashram in Sikkim, where I've come down for rest and recuperation"

"What are you doing there, rest and recuperation is a bit silly."

"Are you surprised?"

She continued, "I needed rest as you remember that after you left you picked me up and dropped me to my apartment and I invited you for a cup of coffee and then that beautiful moment took place between us. You can't forget it."

"But we met at the temple."

"Don't talk nonsense we never met in any temple. We were in my house in my room."

"Can you explain?" I asked

There was no reply and the click told me she had dropped the line.

I realized that I had been part of a great mystery which had been created by the supernatural. Perhaps what happened was a hallucination but what had happened in Yamini apartment was the absolute truth. I just sat and stared at the hills outside my window.

YAMINI

I am going to tell you the story of Yamini. What an exotic name what does it mean? Yamini was the daughter of Daksha Prajapati, and was won the one of the wives of Kasaypa. Many will be wondering who was Daksha Prajapat? Well friends, Daksha is one of the Prajapati, who is the agent of creation as well as the divine king also known as king Rishi. This beautiful girl in Hindu mythology was the daughter of this king. Yamini also means night, and that means twilight and darkness with twinkling stars and the moon shining in the sky. Who was Kasaypa? he is the Vedic sage of Hinduism and one of the seven ancient sages of the Rig Veda.

I have spent a few moments giving you details of this name because this is a secret name and I happened to have come across this name and the girl in a meeting which is perhaps ordained by God.

The story begins when I drove down into the hills. It was a route which was well known to me and one which I had travelled almost every day for close to a decade. I was familiar with the road, but frankly, I was not aware that there was the temple hidden by a clump of trees which I discovered by accident, despite having driven the road for almost a decade. The temple was not very big. That was the reason it remained hidden from my vision.

It was raining heavily, and the visibility has been reduced to zero and the wipers of the car were running at full speed and yet I couldn't see a thing. Visibility beyond the windscreen was nil. With this situation, I thought it best to stop for some time. I pulled up in front of a clump of trees. I had been seeing this clump for many years. It was a thick clump, and I was sure to get protection from the rain here. I got down from his car and then realized that this was not perhaps the best place to save myself. It could be dangerous because lightning was flashing across the sky, and I had read of cases of people taking shelter under a tree being hit by lightning and so I was alert and started looking around for a better place to save myself. The rain continued to beat on the earth, taking all decisions out of my hand.

I looked around and despite the poor visibility and the heavy rain falling, I could make out that just behind the clump of trees was a temple. I decided the blessed place could be a refuge for me come from the elements of nature. I estimated the distance to be about 10 m and I am moved towards the temple. I negotiated the thick undergrowth and low and behold, I was standing before the temple. The rain had now picked up and it had turned into a thunderstorm; lightning was flashing across the sky and thunder boomed again and again. I thought it best to spend time in the temple till the storm abated. I reached the temple and saw that it was not large, yet I sensed that it was hundreds of years old. It was in a delipidated condition, but I was safe in the foyer of the temple. I had a look inside the sanctum sanatorium and could see the image of Lord Shiva and I realized that this was the temple dedicated to the creator, and the destroyer in Hinduism.

I was wondering what would happen next. I was surprised when a heard a cough of a girl. I looked around but couldn't see anybody. This was because of an optical illusion as the outside was relatively bright and inside dark. I went inside the temple; it was a spontaneous decision and without thinking I entered the temple. My eyes took a moment to adjust to the darkness inside. I could make out the statue of Lord Shiva looking down on me and then I was in for a shock for standing next to the godly figure was a beautiful girl and I was even more shocked to realize that she was the same girl who had met me in the Publishers office way back in Chennai. I recognized the beautiful girl who was now wearing a lovely sari tied low down that accentuated her slim waist.

"Yamini," I asked," what the hell are you doing here?"

She did not reply immediately, but after a moment said," I don't know"

"But I had met you in Egmore"

"I really don't know. The last, I remember is that I was in Egmore in my office and from there I had gone with you to my apartment and now I find myself here."

"It is not possible" I said," such thing happens only in fantasy or in mythology."

"I agree, but we are both of us going through this experience."

I thought for a moment then replied," I can't see anything, but I remember that Arasu your boss was sitting on the table and facing me, and you had entered with the files, and I must say I liked you very much but how come you're here"

"I do not know," she replied." but I understand you are a follower of Lord Krishna, and his color is blue, and it is possible, he is the one who has sent me here."

"It's not possible."

"You may be wrong"

I thought the girl is making a fool of me and I said," this is a lot of bullshit. I am pretty sure you came by Air India and then you took a taxi or something and came here to this God forsaken temple."

She was silent for a moment and then I asked," what next? Do you really believe what you told me that you didn't know anything, and you just materialized at this place?"

"I don't know what to say"?

I was now confused and wondering whether what was happening was a dream or reality. I looked at the sky. It had turned blue and that was a bit of a surprise because the thunder is gone, and it was all so beautiful.

"Listen, Yamini, "I said," don't make a fool of me. I remember we sat in your editor's office, and we discussed my book and suddenly now you appear before me. I'm sure you came here from Chennai, and you must have known about my movements. Frankly I don't believe whatever you are talking."

Yamini paused for a moment and then said," sir I am here and as surprised as you I had gone to sleep and then I got up and I found myself here in the foyer of the temple"

All I could say was," bullshit"

The sky, which had cleared up, once again darkened and clouds began to cover the sky, and thunder crashed across the heavens, and once more, the heavy downpour commenced. Then an electrifying moment took place; lightning crashed and hit a tree in the compound of the temple, just about 30 feet away from where we were standing. There was a crackling sound as the tree caught fire and the resultant smoke and sound frightened Yamini who rushed to me, and I held in my arms and that is the time I realized what a bundle she was, so warm and alive.

"Come closer," I whispered.

I pulled the pulsating girl towards me, and as I enveloped her, I could hear the beating of her heart as it was thumping loudly. Something strange happened next which I cannot explain because I began to kiss Yamini and she reciprocated and the back of my mind, I was wondering what the hell is going on but the crashing all around and holding the girl close to me dulled my thinking capability. I had no time to think, but then Yamini probably realized what was happening and she pushed me away and began to run away, but she slipped and fell on the grass outside and now the rain was beating on her. She tried to cover her face with her arms to escape the rain pouring on her.

I quickly remove my shirt with the intention of covering her and went over, but she looks so lovely and with the rain beating on her with the blouse and saree clinging to her body, bringing out her beauty in relief and I am mesmerized. I am overwhelmed by the sight, and I hover over her and begin to kiss her. I can't stop and kiss her again and again. The rain is falling all around, and it begins to beat on my back, but I don't mind. I am overtaken by desire, and unbutton her blouse and push up her bra, baring her nipples to my sight. I began to suckle them like a child, and after a moment go over to her lips covering her completely, so that rain is beating on my back. One thing leads to another, and now I am conscious, I have moved to the altar of her beauty and find my face hidden there with the rain beating down. This is the decisive moment, and a little later I possess her. The storm is now getting violent and again, lightning hits a stump a hundred yards away. This was the moment and Yamini gave a small yelp like a puppy and I knew that her state had changed from girl to woman.

Much later, I got up and carried her inside the temple which was well protected from the rain and continued kissing her, and then I began to feel anger and close my eyes and I do not know what happened because I fell asleep.

You all know the story of the Rip Van Winkle the man who went to sleep and slept for 20 years. It is something similar only I didn't sleep for 20 years but I got up very shortly after a nap and looked around, but Yamini had vanished, and I was wondering what happened and where she had gone? perhaps I thought she had gone back to Chennai.

I shouted her name, but there was no response. The rain continued and after waiting for almost an hour the rain stopped and I went to my SUV and sat in the seat and wondered what happened. I had no explanation at all.

I put my SUV into gear and the vehicle moved forward, but at the same time I felt lighthearted, and I wondered why. I was wondering how the girl from Chennai had materialized in the temple in front of me and then vanished. I left the temple and continued along the slow winding road back home. I went to my apartment and from there I immediately dialed the Chennai number of my Publisher. He came online and I asked him, "Listen pal, where is Yamini?"

"Very much here"

"Are you sure?"

"Absolutely"

I switched off the mobile and at the same time decided that I am go down to Chennai to investigate what had happened but as I was just getting into bed, I had a call from my director, and he told me that I had to come to America to discuss the layoffs of few people as the Covid epidemic had got out of hand.

I never made it to Chennai and after two months, I returned to India. As I entered, my mobile rang and I switched it on, and I was absolutely thrilled that it was Yamini.

"Is that you?" I asked

"Yes," she replied, "it's me."

"From where you are talking?"

"I am talking from an Ashram in Sikkim, where I've come down for rest and recuperation"

"What are you doing there, rest and recuperation is a bit silly."

"Are you surprised?"

She continued, "I needed rest as you remember that after you left you picked me up and dropped me to my apartment and I invited you for a cup of coffee and then that beautiful moment took place between us. You can't forget it."

"But we met at the temple."

"Don't talk nonsense we never met in any temple. We were in my house in my room."

"Can you explain?" I asked

There was no reply and the click told me she had dropped the line.

I realized that I had been part of a great mystery that had been created by the supernatural. Perhaps what happened was a hallucination but what had happened in Yamini's apartment was the absolute truth. I just sat and stared at the hills outside my window.

FACE OF PASSION

I am reminded of an incident, when was a Flight Lieutenant. This is an important rank in the Air Force and the stepping stone to higher ranks and positions. I was detailed to undergo the Personal Selection Officer Course at the Directorate of Psychological Research, Ministry of Defense. It was a four-week course and very interesting because we were taught how to psychologically assess a candidate for his selection to the Indian Air Force.

After the course was over, we awaited our posting orders. We would take charge of new places. The orders were expected within four weeks. I remember I was posted to the Calcutta Recruiting Centre. I was not very happy about it, and in the evening, I called on one of my mentors, a senior officer from the South, who had been my godfather for a long time in the Service. I will tell you that his name was Santa Claus. This is the name I gave him because Santa Claus in Christian mythology, is a man who dishes out gifts and this senior officer of mine was in the same class.

As my posting orders were out, I decided to call on him in the evening. I had met the wife of Santa Claus a few times earlier at many officer's mess parties. The lady always struck me as a very exciting woman. She was slim with a flat belly proportionately accentuated by her small breasts.

Over the glass of whiskey, I told Santa Claus that I had been posted to the recruiting Centre at Calcutta and was not happy about it. He was a little surprised and asked," How come you don't like Calcutta."

"No," replied, "I don't like this job, and I was wondering as there's another vacancy for an Assistant Provo Marshall and whether I could take up that position."

After a few moments, he twirled his mustache and said," I will do the magical trick for you. I'm going to talk to the DPO tomorrow. Let's see."

That was the end of the meeting, and I said goodbye and left. I observed that Mrs. Santa Claus was looking at me very curiously. The fact is the more I saw her the more I liked her.

Nothing much happened and I took charge of my position at Calcutta and then there was a scandal in the Provo Unit and the OC had to be removed. I got a call from Santa Claus, and he told me that very soon he would talk to the DPO about my move to the Provo Unit as the OC.

The order duly came and was a surprise to other officers working along with me.

I took charge of the provost unit and had to attend the quarterly APM conference in Delhi at Air Headquarters. I proceeded to attend it. After the first day, I rang up Santa Claus and thanked him for what he had done for me.

"Okay, okay, flight," He replied, "Come home for a drink."

"When do I come?"

"Why not tomorrow evening?}

"Okay, Sir," I replied

I came back to my quarters and decided to go to the washroom. The orderly disturbed me with the words, "Sir, there is a telephone call for you."

"Okay," I replied," I'll come and receive it."

There was a common telephone at the end of the corridor of the Barack, and I went across in my nightgown and attended the call

I was surprised to hear the voice of Mrs. Santa Claus.

"How are you?" she asked.

"I'm fine. how are you?"

She continued, "I believe he suggested that you come tomorrow to our place. I'm afraid he may not be there tomorrow, so I suggest why don't you come right now?"

I thought for a moment, and then spontaneously said, "Okay, ma'am, I'm coming."

I took an autorickshaw and reached the Central Vista mess where he was staying. I knocked on the door. A young maid opens the door and ushers me into the drawing room.

I sat on the sofa and wondered whether the Santa Claus would come. I was in for a bit of a surprise because it was not Santa Claus, but Mrs. Santa Claus entered. My breath went away when I saw that she was wearing a beautiful low sari, but no blouse and clad only in a lacy blue color bra.

I was in some turmoil at the sight, and I will say that Mrs. Santa Claus looked ravishing. My eyes riveted on her bust, and I was wondering what the game was.

She said," I have just dismissed the maid because she wants to go away, and I will make you a cup of tea."

"Where is Sir?" I asked.

She smiled and said," he's not here, as he has to go to a meeting."

I was a little intrigued but decided not to question the matter further because Santa was someone special to me.

She returned with a cup of tea and biscuits, and two Samosas, so obviously she had prepared, for my visit. He served me tea and while serving, the cloth covering her bust slipped down and I was witness to Mrs. Santa Claus only in her lingerie.

It was the month of June and very hot, and though the fan was running at full speed, it could not lower the temperature. I was wondering what was going on, and I told myself to keep steady man, keep steady

Mrs. Santa Claus smiled and said," You know something, Lieutenant, I have always liked you."

"But I said what about Santa Claus"

"He is fine. He said he's on temporary duty now and won't be coming back for two days, so he had asked me to tell you this."

"But he called me tomorrow."

Yes, he did, but this is the message he had given, and since he was not here, I thought it best for you to come in his absence."

"The heat is oppressive," she said, and let the pallu fall to the ground on the Carpet. Mrs. Santa Claus looked pretty in the bra.

"When it is hot," she says," it rains, and I hope it rains now."

I was wondering what to reply, but as of on cue, I could hear the crash of thunder outside, and the rain began to fall on the earth, and I could hear the dull sound as it fell on the earth.

Another crash of thunder and I don't know how, Mrs. Santa Claus, just fell into my lap. I do not know if it was by accident or preplanned. All the same, she was in my lap and her soft flesh pressed against me. She was wearing an exotic perfume. I gently kissed her shoulder, and then another crash of lightning and thunder hitting the earth decided the future course of events. I pulled the straps of her bra down and kissed the bare nipples. I picked her up and entered her bedroom and laid her on the bed. What followed was a hedonistic delight as I kissed her body and soon a crash of thunder coincided with my victory. Before that, I had raised her to a pitch and her body trembled like a leaf in a storm. I remember my face at the altar of her beauty, and we were oblivious to the thunder cashing across the sky. At the back of my mind, I realized I was not using any protection and I was wondering how it happened or did Mrs. Santa wish it that way. A hidden meaning?

I left the house after the rain and went back to the mess

On reaching my mess, I found a message for me, this was handed to me by the bellboy. It was from Santa Claus and said, 'I'm proceeding on urgent duty to Secunderabad, so would I come and meet him on my next trip to Delhi?

I patted the back of the boy and said," Thank you for the information." and went back to my apartment. I was wondering what happened. I never went back the next day to the residence of Santa Claus, though I had a telephone call from Mrs. Santa Claus to come over for another cup of tea

When I got into the east command, Courier an AN-12, I looked out of the window of the plane and saw the beautiful clouds and the clear blue sky. I smiled at the events, that had taken place and realized it was not something created by me, it was the will of God. The Courier was proceeding to Bagdogra, and I got down there and took a train to Calcutta. Now this incident remains a fleeting memory. I wonder if it was a Xmas gift for me. Santa Claus well, he had always given me gifts. I don't know but the Lord Krishna says that *on this earth, not a leaf moves without my will.*

CHAPTER THREE

GODS GIFT

I will narrate an extraordinary tale and wonder whether it was a mystic experience, a reality, or a figment of my imagination. I had been asked to move from Bagdogra to Jammu and put in charge of a fighter squadron. War clouds were hovering and my squadron was slated to go into battle. Jammu is very close to the temple of the Goddess Durga. I decided to visit there before entering combat, so I took my SUV and began the drive. I wanted to pay my respects and return quickly because in the morning I was supposed to take off in a sortie to scour the enemy in the Hills.I drove slowly through the hills, and then I stopped because on the left side stood a beautiful girl with a small bag. I was a little surprised seeing her and asked her how come she was standing here like this.

"Sir," the girl replied," I was traveling by bus, but the bus had a flat tire and we all got down I had just gone to the bushes to relieve myself and when I returned I found the bus had left without me.

"I scratched my head and wondered whether she was telling the truth because generally, the drivers take all passengers with them. But still, when I saw the girl and her mesmerizing beauty, I hoped she was telling the truth. She had her sari tied below the navel of her belly and looked

lovely. "Okay," I said," get in the front seat; where do you want to go? "She looked at me and said I would like to go to the temple of the Goddess Durga, but before that can we drive along this road to a small temple.
"Okay," I replied, "no harm in that."

I put my car into gear and we began to move up the hill. It's a steep hill and the engine was puffing away in second gear. Soon the temple came to sight and she said "Stop."
I stopped the vehicle and she got down and went inside the temple. I kept sitting in my SUV, waiting for her. A good 15 minutes passed, and the girl didn't come out of the temple and I was wondering what's happened. I decided to check and got down from the SUV and went inside the temple. It was a small temple but I was in for a shock because inside the temple, there was nobody. I wondered where the girl had vanished. I noticed a small door at the back and I thought she might have gone out of the door but I was wondering why she went out of the door and why she didn't come back to the SUV.
I wanted to shout for her, but then I realized that I didn't even know her name so I shouted," Girl, girl where are you?." My voice echoed in the hills and could be heard miles away but then I wondered what had happened and I wanted to go back to my SUV. I thought the girl had run away but somehow my mind was not convinced and I was wondering if something strange would happen, for the simple reason the girl was so beautiful and I admit it fuelled my imagination. I was wondering what to do and thought calm myself by praying.

I sat before the deity of Lord Shiva, closed my eyes, and began to pray. I thought I would pay my obeisance and then continue to the temple. I got up to leave when I heard a rustle, and I was taken aback to see the girl enter inside through the door. Well, I thought that solved the mystery. She had gone out of the door to her village and come back. But I had nagging doubts because the girl had an aura about her, and it was not like a village girl would have. But what surprised me, was the girl who entered before me was attired in another dress. She had the exotic saree and a blouse that just got so low there was nothing much to hide. She had lovely eyes and a smooth complexion, and I couldn't accept that this girl could be from the village. I would more likely relate her to a high-class family because she looked more like a princess.

The girl came, placed her hands on my shoulders, and said," Capt. God has decided to give you a gift."

"What gift?"

"You will find out soon enough."

"But what about this gift?" The girl smiles and says, "You are a warrior, a Kshatriya, and tomorrow you are going to battle, and today god will give you something which you will cherish, and a person will come into your life. I will give you a ring, that will bring you good luck in the battle tomorrow. The gods have noted great danger to you."

I was not impressed, and asked," Why should God be impressed with me, I am living my life happily."

"Yes," she said, "you are a man of God, a man of principle, and in the true sense like Arjuna, a great warrior. The gods have seen your life and noted that many times you spared the enemy so that he could survive. You are a man of chivalry, and I am pretty sure you deserve your gift."

"OK," I said, "but where is the gift?" She bent forward, kissed my eyes, and whispered, "I am the gift."

As it happened, there was a crash of thunder, and it began to rain heavily outside, and here I was with this beautiful girl in the small temple of Shiva. I looked out of the door and saw the rain beating on the earth, and the visibility was greatly reduced. I could see my SUV but became invisible because of the thick fog coming up. The girl kept looking at me and gently kissed me on my lips. I thought this girl was cooking a tale about the gods and the gift. I thought she was a lonely girl and maybe looking for an outlet for her energy. But the more I saw her, the more I realized that beauty was ethereal, her eyes, deep and blue, warm lips and aquiline nose, slender neck, and then her bust so beautiful that one wonders what they would look if they were free.

The girl kissed me once more and ran out of the back door into the rain "Look," I said," don't go into the rain. It can be trouble. You could get a chill. "Outside, the rain was beating heavily on the earth, and when I looked out of the door, I couldn't see the girl, and then I saw her just a few feet away, and she was drenched, and this added to her sexiness.

I shouted above the noise of the thunder and the rain," Immediately come inside," She just looked and didn't answer.

"Okay," I said," I'm coming."

I was concerned for the girl in the rain and stepped out and soon reached her, gathered her in my arms, and began to walk back to the temple. She sneezed, and that was cause for concern. I wondered what to say when she did something that took my breath away. "I am wet," she said," and I don't want to get a chill". She followed up by opening the buttons of her blouse and taking it off. She was not wearing a bra, and her breast's beauty captivated me. She softly whispered, "Come, just touch me," I couldn't wait any longer and slowly brought my hand and touched her breast. I caressed her breast like she was a porcelain doll. "touch me," she whispered. Emboldened, I unraveled her sari. It fell in a heap at her feet. I gently lifted her and placed her on the floor, parted her thighs to witness her esoteric delight. I spread the folds, buried my face, and sought her innermost recess. The rain continued, and there was thunder and lightning. She paid her tribute, and now I was a tiger. I closed my eyes and was bewildered, I saw myself flying, and following me was the enemy fighter, OH god, what's happening.! The taste, smell, and feel of her so close to me, skin to skin, time and space, had no meaning anymore. There was only her. I closed my eyes and again saw the enemy fighter. He was behind me, and he fired his guns. The salvo almost hit me, and now I think, I will lose. What's happening? I opened my eyes and realized I was on top of the beauty. I thrust into her.

As I close my eyes, I see myself in the plane and realize I'm lucky there was not much damage, and I decided the time had come to do the cobra Manoeuvre. I put my plane in a 90° vertical climb, which surprised the enemy, and I was behind him and fired my guns, I hit his plane, and I could see the pilot eject. I didn't want to hurt him, and I flew back to base. As I landed, the ground-crew, rushed and helped me out and said," Sir, you put in a great fight". I am bewildered because I remember I was in the temple making love to the most beautiful woman in the world. Was it all a fantasy? I cannot tell as the aircrew van drove to the base operations room. However, I looked at my hand and saw the ring on my finger. What did it mean

CHAPTER FOUR

THE NAXALITE

THE NAXALITE

Mary was an Indian Christian and she had joined the Indian police service. She was posted for a six-month tenure in the Naxalite-infested area of Chhattisgarh. She took charge as the assistant superintendent. As she joined duty, her senior warned her to avoid going too deep into the forest unless it was a combing operation with armed police. She obeyed the instructions, but the Almighty has a hand in everything.

One evening, when returning from patrol Mary, 3 of her guards found a roadblock; a large tree had been placed on the small road. While she kept sitting in the jeep two men got down to lift the tree so the jeep could pass. Suddenly a shot rang in the air and about 15, Naxalites some armed with automatic rifles came out from the jungle. The entire party was taken by surprise and they couldn't do anything. It would have been a disaster. The men moved towards the jeep and seeing the girl said to the men "You are lucky you are with a lady and we are not going to kill you now, but we will take you to our boss. As far as you are concerned. Feel lucky that you have survived."

They disarmed the guards took Mary's revolver and walked about 3 km into the jungle, Mary was surprised to see that they had been taken to a small camp. The men were taken away and put in one of the tents and she presumed they would be kept there. One of the men said, "Please come and meet the Chief."

She was taken into another tent, and after her eyes got acclimatized to the light, she saw a man sitting in the chair. She was surprised he was young, About 27. He had a flowing beard and a fair complexion.

The man arose from his chair and said," I am surprised that a lady police officer has been sent to us.'

Mary didn't say anything.

The man continued, "You are lucky because we will not kill you though the police have killed some of our women combatants."

Hostage

Mary could make out the man's demeanour was chic, and she wondered what he was doing in the jungle

He clapped his hands and shouted, "Get 2 cups of tea". He turned to the girl and said, "Sit down on the chair."

Mary had been feeling tired after the jungle trek and thankfully sat down

"What are you going to do with me?" She asked.

"Nothing, you will be a hostage here".

A boy entered with 2 cups of tea. There were also some biscuits on a plate. He put the tray on the small wooden table and left. The man got up from his chair, and Mary noticed he was extremely fit. He picked up one cup and handed it to Mary.

"I hope you have not drugged it," Mary asked.

" Why should I, you are my prisoner; drink the tea. It is good Assam tea, something that I like and miss the Assam tea plantations.

"Were you there before?"

"Yes, I was the manager of one of the estates in Silchar before I joined the Communist movement."

"Do you think you did the right thing?"

"I do not know because I have so many doubts in my mind now and I realize we will not be able to defeat the government. Perhaps if we come out in the open and fight an electoral battle would be better but at the moment your police are hunting for me and I have a reward of ₹ 100,000 on my head."

"You are not scared."

"Not at all and I don't mind dying but of course, I do miss the days when I was in Calcutta."

"What were you doing in Calcutta?"

"I was studying there at the Calcutta University. I did my PhD in philosophy."

Mary was bewildered, how could a highly educated man take to fighting the government in a guerilla war, in which there was very little chance of their winning?

She sipped the tea and found it was good and welcome. She looked at the man and said," Why did you leave Calcutta?"

"You know my parents are there and they don't know I am in Chhattisgarh. My name is MN Roy and revolution is in my blood. The Communist Party of India has made common cause with the government and joined them but I feel a revolution is ripe in Chhattisgarh where the tribals are exploited."

"You seem to be an intellectual."

"No, not at all. I'm a very lethal man and I killed many of the policemen in encounters but now I feel it is better to give up this life."

"Will you give it up?"

"No, because if I do somebody from the cadre will kill me because they would consider my decision a betrayal and so I must continue.'

"It is getting dark, and where am I going to sleep."

"In my tent."

"I can't sleep with a man in the same room."

Roy smiled and said, "You have no choice, and rest assured I do not believe in molesting any woman because if I put you in another tent, my men can get other ideas. We are rarely able to capture a woman police officer and I must say you're beautiful."

"What about clothes I don't have any"

" I will give you a Ghagra and a blouse and ask one of our women guards to come and give them to you He whistled, perhaps it was a call sign and a woman entered. I could make out that she was short and young. She came in and seeing Mary asked, "What can I do?"

"Would you give her a Ghagra and blouse to change and take her to the loo?"

"After everything was over, Mary came and sat down in the tent She wore the Ghaghra and the blouse the girl had given. She had also asked her to remove her underclothes. "No," Mary had resisted," I don't want to do these things."

The girl replied, "We have a woman who does the washing, she will wash your clothes as well."

She is sitting in the tent with the Ghagra and the blouse but without underclothes, wondering what will happen. She was not scared and decided she would fight anything that happened to her.

Roy entered the 1tent and said, " I could never imagine you are so beautiful. The Ghagra fits you wonderfully and the blouse is so beautiful it accentuates your beauty"

"Don't talk like this," she said," I am your enemy and hostage."

"I am beginning to wonder whether you are an enemy because I have a feeling ultimately you will be on our side."

"I will never take part in any killing."

"But you came here for a tenure, and that includes killing us"

He paused and continued, "It's time for dinner. I will eat dinner with my men but somebody will bring yours. Maybe one of the girls will bring dinner for you. I hope you will be thankful." With these words, Roy left with the words, " It is pretty late now." One of the guards entered with a tray. Mary had been feeling hungry for a long time and was excited to see the rice and the fish curry with the onion salad. she relished the meal or maybe she was in a position where she was hungry and eager to satisfy her need.

After she is finished, she wants to go out with the tray and leave it. As she stepped out of the tent she found a guard there and he said," Don't leave, you remain in the tent." Meanwhile, the girl who brought the tray took the empty tray back and Mary came back and settled in the chair

She observed, there was one bed more like a camp cot, which is part of the kit given to Officers of the Police. Roy entered and asked, "I hope you like the meal."

"Yes, it was not bad but you must be careful. The news of my kidnapping would have gone to headquarters and a battalion of the police would be searching for me and my three men. What are you going to do with them."

"Nothing, they are lucky with you. I'm going to put them in our Jeep and leave them miles away from this place in the jungle and they will have to fend for themselves and perhaps they will reach the camp but they will not know where we are because I will blindfold them while taking them away."

"Thank you for their lives," Mary said, "but what are you going to do with me?"

" I don't know. You are so beautiful almost like a doll. I don't know why you wore the uniform, you would be much better off in Bombay films."

He continued, "You know the famous actress Piety Zinta, you remind me of her and I'm glad you're so lovely, which part of India are you from?"

" Madras"

"Then you are a Brahmin convert because it is only the Brahmin girls who are so fair. you remember Jayalalitha?"

Mary did not answer.

Roy continued, "I will be sleeping on the floor here and you can sleep on the bed, but I think we can chat philosophy."

"Which part of India are you from?" Mary asked though she knew what he had told her that he was a Bengali.

Roy replied, "You already know, I told you I am from Calcutta and I miss Calcutta, Park Street, Chowranghee, and all the places there.

"Why don't you surrender and go back?"

"No way, I will fight to the end because somebody must fight for the poor tribals who are exploited."

They were into an animated conversation and she realized that Roy was an extremely knowledgeable man. They talked about everything politics, Plato, Aristotle, free love land they had passed valuable time. Roy looked at his watch and said, "Can you imagine we have been talking for four hours?"

Mary kept quiet, but she was impressed with the man.

He just smiled and said," I can see you are so beautiful,"

Three days passed, and one day Roy told her, "Your three men have been set free 50 miles from this place, they were blindfolded and taken there and left."

"What about me?"

"Do you want to escape? you tell me."

"If you want to go, you're free to go but bear in mind that for me, you are the most precious thing in the world. The most beautiful girl I've ever seen."

"Why do you say that?"

"I wonder if I should tell you."

"Yes, tell me"

"I have seen you naked when you were changing clothes in this tent from a small window and believe me, I have never seen a more beautiful girl than you. I don't want to keep you against your wish but I hope you will stay."

Suddenly a clap of thunder hit the sky and rain began to fall. There was a flash and a loud sound as lightning hit a tree nearby. Mary clutched Roy. It was something she didn't intend, but Roy had gathered her in his arms and began to kiss her.

"Stop it," she said. She liked the man and the philosophical talk they had been having and she knew he was not an ordinary man. His tongue probed deep into her mouth and Mary was wondering what was going to happen. "Please Mary," he said," I see Lord Krishna has made you. Outside, there is thunder and lightning and all the men would be in the tents, but you come with me into the rain."

Mary did not know what to say, and soon he had gathered her in his arms, and then she realized his prodigious strength. The raindrops were falling, and she was cradled in his arms, her lips were glued to him, and soon her blouse had become wet and clung to her body. Her Ghaghra highlighted her body and its charms.

Roy took her to a small patch of grass. There was nobody around and he laid her on the soft grass and opened the buttons of her blouse. He circumscribed her breasts now bear with his tongue and the saliva spread all over them. He did it repeatedly and then suckled her nipples. The rain was falling and Mary was wet. It was heavy rain something she had never experienced. His other hand was now moving down and he was loosening the cord that bound her ghagra and pulling it down, The lord had bared all her treasures to him.

He traced an exotic pattern with his tongue, while the rain continued to fall on both of them, and Mary found that she had put his face between her thighs. He was licking as if his life depended on it and she reached orgasm. How many she could never count, the rain continued to fall, and it was a hedonistic delight, she was conscious that he had taken her. It was much better than the last time she had sex with a college friend who had been Boorish. He was gentle and so understanding. She had reached a pitch with his tongue and she had already orgasmed twice, and now she was willing to receive him. The rain continued to fall and now he had covered her completely and she was safe as it fell on his back. It was the beast in him that came up and soon she felt an orgasm as she was floating in the heavens, she had forgotten about the rain and it was over and he lay painting on of her. The next three days were spent in total bliss and soon the second in command came to Roy and said

"Sir, I think you have forgotten about the revolution. My advice is to kill the girl now and move from the area because the police will be coming here soon."

Roy thought for a moment, "No, he said we are not going to kill. No purpose will be served. But yes, we should move from this camp, pack up, and move."

He looked at Mary and said, "My darling. I'm going to set you free. I will show you the path it's not very far. Your police have no idea of the jungle. We are very close to your camp. you can .go"

"What about you?"

"I will go with my men to another place."

She wanted to say I want to come with you, but the words never came to her lips.

He sensed what she wanted to say and replied. "Don't worry get transferred to Calcutta. I will come there."

She found the camp dismantled in 15 minutes and they were all moving away, and Roy came to her kissed her, and said," You go straight, here is a compass, for 3 miles then turn right and you will reach the camp and we will become invisible in the jungle."

Mary left and soon she was at the Police camp. There was a lot of hue and cry. People were asking where she had been and whether she had been tortured, She didn't reply but made her report to the IG. In the report, she stated that a general amnesty be given to all the rebels. The IG read the report and was irritated. He wrote," The tenure of the officer is over and she is transferred to Calcutta."

A painting of a person
hugging a person Description
automatically generated

She reached Calcutta and took charge, but things were moving very fast and once when she was sitting in the chair, she felt uneasy and realized she had missed two periods. She got a test done and it was confirmed that she was pregnant. She was sitting in the chair wondering what was going to happen. Roy belongs to Calcutta. He studied at Calcutta University. If Roy came to know that she was with child he would leave and come to Calcutta. She sat in the chair closed her eyes and wondered what will happen. She had a feeling that he would soon be coming. She kept waiting but Roy never came. A year later she was perusing some old files and she read that a notorious Naxalite had been killed in an encounter. She dare not read the name. She closed the file with a thumping heart and wiped her brow, now wet with perspiration.

CHAPTER FIVE

MEMORIES

I am reminded of an incident almost 2 decades back. At that time as a youngster, I dreamed of many things and one of those was making love to an American girl, a pure white girl. One can say, it was a stupid fantasy in a way it was, but I had a fixation after watching so many Hollywood actresses at that time including Jennifer O'Neal and Jacqueline Bisset. Two decades passed in (Service) and the dream faded away in between I had an affair with a Russian girl and the American dream was put in cold storage. But Krishna has a strange way of looking after his believers. As a wing commander at 42, I was asked to proceed to America along with the Air Staff Inspection team. It was to be a visit for 10 days and we were to study the American method of inspections by interacting with the American Air team.

I will not mention the bases where we went except to say that we landed at a prominent Air Defence Centre and very soon briefings began. After the first briefing was over I came out and one of the Lt Cols of the American Airforce asked me if he could be of any help. I thought for a moment and then replied ," I love motorbike driving, and I wanted a motorbike to move around the country."

He replied, "I can give you Harley but friend, you won't be able to go very far because you're in a course. Yeah, and you have to be attending classes also as well as a briefing."

"I won't go very far," I replied," just around the camp and maybe a few kilometres into the countryside."

He said," That's fine, come with me."

He gave me a Harley, the fat boy. I hadn't driven a Harley earlier, and he told me not to worry because it's a powerful machine. All I had to do was to keep looking at the road and take care of myself and the bike would take care of me..

I asked him if I could start straight away

"Yes," he replied, " you can come back for the dinner because we are going to have a dining-in-night today You know it's an important ceremonial occasion and it's important that both teams raise a toast to our cooperation."

"Don't worry," I replied

I drove to the guardroom and a beautiful girl, perhaps a corporal came out. Her beauty smote me. She was slim and her rank badges were on her shoulders. She was fair and slender with long legs. She was the most enticing thing I've seen in a long time, she came up to me to check my identity card and mentioned," You come from India?"

"Yes," I replied," we will stay here for 10 days."

"That is so nice," she replied, "I have not been to India but heard a lot about it and the beautiful monument, The Taj Mahal."

After a moment, she asked me," Where are you going?

"No where just driving around the place."

"You know the roads," she asked

"No," I replied, "but my GPS will guide me."

"That means you have no fixed agenda"

"That is right"

She thought and said," Sir, my duty is over. Can you drop me at my apartment and then you can drive off."

My heart was beating so fast that I feared it was going to burst out of my breast. "Yes," I replied, "it is a great pleasure."

"Will you wait a moment and I'll change to Mufti and be back in a minute."

I switched off the Harley's engine and waited. She came out in a lovely short skirt and blouse, and I could make out the girl was lovely, I was wondering if such a girl must have a lot of boyfriends.

She sat in the back, and I started the bike and moved out. "Where do you want to go? "I asked.

"I will give you the directions" " she said," take me to my apartment and drop me there."

I was driving the bike and the girl was sitting at the back. She was giving me instructions. After about 15 minutes of driving, we reached a set of houses and she said," You can stop here and I will get off."

I stopped the Harley and she popped off the machine and headed towards the door about 10 feet away. I thought I should make the first move and told the girl," I need some payment for dropping you here"

"Payment," she was surprised.

I laughed and said," You could call me for coffee."

"Sir, you are an officer and I am an NCO. Normally officers are not supposed to fraternise with NCOs."

I laughed. "Don't make that an excuse for not inviting me for coffee. "Any case, nobody is here to see that an officer like me is dining with an NCO." She signaled with her hand for me to come, and I put the bike on its stand and moved towards the NCO.

"What's your name?" I asked.

"Sally," she replied

"Okay, Sally," I said," I hope you're going to make a good cup of coffee"

She smiled and I could make out that her smile was wonderful and she put the key in the lock, opened the door and went inside. It was a small apartment, but very well kept, and then she went into the kitchen to make coffee.

She came out with 2 cups handed one to me and said," Please drink it. I hope you like it."

I sipped the coffee and told her," It's nice as good as you are."

"What do you mean?"

"I mean that you are beautiful and I suppose you have a lot of boyfriends."

"No," she replied, "I don't have boyfriends because I have a condition"

"What is that?"

"I will be the friend of any boy who can beat me in sword fencing.'

"That is something silly."

"It's my fixation."

"Are you a fencer?

" Yes, It's a sport I love and have several wonderful poniard's."

"Yes, it is a wonderful sport, but I haven't played it any time."

"Would you like to play now?"

"Well, I don't mind. I suppose it is pretty harmless."

She smiled, and said," No it is not harmless. You can lose some blood as well."

I felt something was wrong and told her," Don't bother. I think I'll go after the coffee."

"You seem to have developed cold feet"

The word stuck like a hammer and I replied," No, I will play the game with you."

She went away and came back in a skimpy dress that put her body to advantage, and there was no doubt that she was the loveliest girl I had ever seen. Maybe she was beautiful because of the sword fencing and the exercises that go with it.

After we drank the coffee, she said," If you pass the fencing, Test, you can stay for dinner. Otherwise, you get on your bike and go home."

I was reminded of my training in the Academy days where I had done a lot of boxing. I remember the Sergeant shouting at me," Singh, I want stronger punches from you."

Sally returned with two swords and she gave one of them to me. "That's a good sword, I have given you. It's one of the best with me. It's very sharp and can draw my blood."

"Are you serious?" I asked.

"You think I'm not serious," she swished her sword in the air and the way she swished showed she was a professional.

I took the sword in my hand and got ready. A 42-year-old man was going to face a 21-year-old girl in a match.

That time I prayed to Lord Krishna and told him to keep my respect. I said I have followed you for the last four decades. Now is the time for you to see that I don't lose. Just then a flower from the photo of Jesus, where I think Sally had put a small garland fell and it looked a little peculiar to me but perhaps this was the signal, the Lord had sent that I could go into battle with this girl.

"Okay," I said," let's go". She came at me and slashed at me with her poniard. I was alert and paired the blow with my hand and the first round was on. She now stood before me and we touched epees together, and she was using her sword to get a break, and I was defending. It was because of military training and the inherent fitness that I held on for some time. Her blows were blunted by me, and then she came, and this time there was a deadly intent in her eyes. I knew that I was going to get into trouble. I decided that I must take the game away from her to my ground and with my superior strength I hit a massive blow to the epee which she held in her hand. Probably she hadn't ever received such a blow and the sword fell from her hand and clattered away some distance. I now placed my poniard at her neck and blouse and pulled it and the blouse came off

"What are you doing? "She said," Let me get my epee back because what you have done is not the correct way to fight."

"For me, it is the correct way," I said

I moved forward and pulled the blouse off. She had small brazier breasts and marvelled at their beauty. "

"You can't do this. This is not part of the game. Give me back my sword and I will teach you a lesson, you will never forget".

"No," I said," you had your chance and you lost and now the ground is mine."

I was overtaken by passion. Perhaps Lord Krishna had come to me. She was wearing a dress that did not stand the pressure of my strength and it gave away, the buttons broke and she was bare. She tried to cover herself. "You haven't played the game fair and Square," she says.

"Well," I said," warriors take what they get."

I did something spontaneously. I just lifted her in my arms went to the adjacent room with the bed and threw her on it. Very soon. I had divested myself of my shirt and trousers and enveloped her in my arms. I kissed her as never before, and suddenly I saw her getting limp.

"Don't" she says.

"It is the law of nature. I am the warrior and you have lost."

She didn't say anything. I did not pull the panty down but put my hand in the elastic and pulled it up. The flimsy garment was not used to such strength and it tore at the seam and Sally was completely nude.

But a strange thing has happened. She will not protest now as I applied my lips to her breast, and began to kiss her. I moved down to the soft curls and soon I heard nothing but her sighs and orgasm as she crossed her legs and around my head.

What followed was a delight into a land where very few go. Very soon I possessed Sally and this time she reciprocated. It was not long before I prayed my tribute to the temple and collapsed, breathing heavily. She had put her arms around me and kissed me and said," You are a very brave man. I have never met anyone like you, but now you stay here."

"But there is a dining-in- night"

"Forget about it. I will not let you go."

The entire night was passed in rare transport of joy. I had in the meanwhile telephoned, the team leader the Air Commodore that I had a stomach ache and was excused from the dining- in- night.

"Not to worry boy,' he said, "we can manage without you."

That night in my 42 years was the most glorious, I've ever spent. It was a dream which I had for two decades and it had been fulfilled. It seemed like I never had enough of Sally and so it continued till the early hours of the morning when exhausted, I went to sleep with Sally curled beside me.

I woke up in the morning and saw Sally still fast asleep. I repeatedly kissed her and told her good morning. She woke up and went to the washroom and came out and said we will have some breakfast now.

I did something very silly. I didn't go back to the camp and it was five days of bliss. I wouldn't let her go for duty also and she agreed. Mind you, we didn't have another fencing match. All the matches we had were either on the couch, the bed, or the rug in the living room. It was just eating, drinking, wine or whiskey, and exploring each other.

As I came into her again, she kissed me and said," I have no protection I don't know what's going to happen."

"Well," I replied, " if something happens, please let me know."

"What will you do?"

"Take you away and make you mine forever"

She left and kissed me

The thought that I would impregnate, thrilled me, and once more, I felt myself rising. Another encore followed and soon six days elapsed and I got a call from my leader. He said," Commander, I have come to know everything. You come back now because I understand your position. Don't worry I'm not going to take any action and we are going back. That is important."

"Thank you very much, sir," I said " But how do you know all this?"

"Commander, I didn't become Commodore if didn't keep track of everything. I know what's happening and goodbye and come back."

I told her I would be going away. She kissed me again and now it was to be the last time and once more I carried her to the bed. This time she looked like a virgin and again

I had gone to the land of love a beautiful place, with flowers and roses all around and I closed my eyes, I could see nothing but the beauty. There were clouds floating and angels singing and maybe it was my imagination but I saw the chariot of Lord Krishna and he was moving across the heavens. I emptied my essence into her and then left. I joined my team. They were inquisitive as to where I had gone. I told them that I had gone to meet some relations and one of them had serious health problems and I couldn't come. The plane took off, and I landed in Agra.

Six months elapsed and I got up in the morning when my telephone rang. I was a little surprised and I looked at the caller ID and the visible number showed this was a call from America. I lifted the receiver, it was the voice of Sally

"You want to know, the result of that beautiful time we spent together."

"Yes, what's happened?

"I'm getting a baby," she said

My heart began to beat fast. I was, a 42 bachelor, and she was 21 and was carrying my baby. What was I supposed to do?

I finish the story here friends and leave you to guess the ending; did I go back and bring her or I just ignore her? Your guess is as good as mine but that will mean another story, so goodbye. Enjoy whatever I have written.

CHAPTER SIX

KAVITA

I have been in love with the woman staying in the opposite flat since I rented my flat. Many times I have noticed her and maybe she has also noticed me looking at her. I keep wondering what she thinks of me. I keep looking at her and my fantasy runs riot. I want to hug her and I fantasize how she would look without clothes. She looks stunning and the dress today is short above the knee, which highlights her legs and a flat belly leaving very little for my imagination. But I've never gotten the courage to talk. to her. Six months have elapsed and I am wondering that perhaps today something will change. Today is December 22nd. What's so special about December 22? Well, it's the longest night of the year and I am hoping that this longest night would be the opening to Alibaba's cave. I can fantasize, about her lovely face and then I close my eyes and I can't help not thinking of the curls on her mons. Does she have them? The thought excites me no end. Would I ever hide my face in that fur and savour the excitement of paying homage with my tongue?

I am hoping it will be a long night. My luck would be changing, I was sure but why was I so confident? I heard the others talking about December 22nd, the longest night of the year. I will have the most time for her tonight, as the daylight takes our movement away.

I come from the office and watch the sunset from my window. It's a beautiful sight as I watch the sky turning beautiful shades of colours. The colours in the sky, as they change are beautiful. Once the sun sets, I will be free to approach her. My day in the Office was passed, anticipating the night and the chance that I would see the woman of my dreams opposite my flat. All day, I have been working and trying to keep my mind on the jobs given to me by my boss. I tried to concentrate on the work, but I couldn't get away from the fantasy appearing before me of the woman in her house and dropping her dress in front of me.

The clock is ticking away and now it is time to pack up and go. Everybody has gone and I am the only person left. My blood pressure is rising; I don't know but I can feel the thumping of my heart as I'm the last man to leave, close the door, and take the elevator down.

I reach my house, open the door, and look out of the window. The sun slips lower and lower along the horizon. I can feel the tingle in my hands as the sun descends. It means that I will soon come to life and I will be able to talk to her. I have been in this flat for around 10 years, but she came 6 months ago. I have never once spoken to her. I have tried, but I can never force myself to start. I want to say hello, but the words get stuck in my throat. I am wondering how I'm going to make my pass to her.

Did I tell you that in my spare time, I paint, yes, I paint on canvas. I have the half-finished painting of the woman in front of me. I Drop the brush and now it's pretty dark and the long night is beginning. I move away from my canvas, but not before I have planted a kiss on the beautiful face, I was painting and then I get up and move to the door. I open it and stand there looking at the opposite flat door.

She has not yet come, but I will keep standing here till she comes. There is an absolute silence all around and no one else is in sight then I hear the elevator coming up and it opens and out she steps. This beautiful girl. She looks at me standing at the door and smiles but doesn't say anything as she puts the key in the lock of the door to open it. I see her framed in the door; somehow the door is not opening and then something strange happens, the keys dropped to the floor and she goes down to pick them up. I'm seized of the moment and I just run to her side. What the hell am I doing? I kneel next to her and pick up the keys. I do not want to hand them to her, for now, I feel these keys are the ones that are going to open Ali Baba's cave. I look at her put the key in the lock and turn it and I can hear the click as the door opens. She's looking at me with a half-smile and she reminds me of a beautiful goddess

"Are you alright?" I ask, my voice low and tender.

"Yes, thank you. So nice that you ran across to pick up the keys, my dress is so tight. I would have difficulty picking them up." Her voice is like a melody. She smiles at me and takes my hand. We stand together, her hand still in mine. Neither of us dare to move. I don't even dare to breathe.

I push open the door and inside the small apartment I notice an old gramophone. I wish she asked me in and then my prayers were answered. She says," Thank you for helping me but why don't you come inside"

Fantasy further

This is the invitation I was waiting for and I quickly move inside and she follows me. I give her the keys and she deposits them on the table and then looks at me and says,

"Do you like my gramophone.?

"Yes, it's lovely it's antique, isn't it?"

"Yes, and I have some old records, would you like me to play them for you?"

"I would love it."

"Okay, I will play them but before that, I will get you a drink. What would you like?"

"Nothing, anything, whatever you're drinking."

"I'm going to take gin and lime"

"Same for me"

There is a lovely bar and she goes there and makes the cocktail and then surprises me by saying, "I have wanted to talk to you for a long time at least for the last six months ever since I saw you in the door."

"You have seen me in the door"

"Yes, every day."

"I will tell you a secret. I have also been watching you; believe me, I have fantasized about many things."

"I can understand," she says with a smile.

Her gaze is warm and comforting, and I melt beneath her stare.

She hands me a glass, and I slowly start sipping it, watching her while I sip. My heart is beating fast and I wonder if this will be my night, my dream night which I have been waiting for the last six months.

"Oh? I wanted to ask you something," I say, looking down at her dress tight and sexy showcasing some of the loveliest legs I have seen. How old could she be 24,25? I am touching half a century.

"Okay," she says I will now play some music. Would you like to listen to some old music from Stef Moeder?"

I didn't know who Steff Moeder was, but replied, "Yes I love this music. Please put it on". She walks to the gramophone, lifts the hood removes a record from a jacket, and sets it on the turntable, then pushes the stylus to the record which begins to turn as she places it on the edge. It's beautiful music that starts playing but maybe I like the music because it's been put on by this girl, my fantasy.

I cannot believe I am listening to a record from a woman whom I have fantasized about for six months. Sometimes I feel that what is happening is unreal. Outside the sun has set and it's a long night and here I am listening to music with a girl that I have fantasized about for the last six months. It feels like a dream.

The record is now playing out soft lilting melodies and she looks at me and says ." I love this music and I love to dance to it."

"Dance to it?"

"Yes, why not?"

"Yes," I say, "Yes, I also want to dance."

We move to the centre of the room, our hands joined together. I don't want to let her go; not now, and not ever. I am imagining we are in a real dance hall and there are lots of people around and the girl is cuddling close to me and everybody's looking at me and wondering look this foggy has got such a hot girl with him. My thoughts are cut and I realize that there are only two of us here.

The woman lets go of my hand, but only for a moment. She takes my other hand in hers and raises them above our heads. My palm presses against hers and I pause. I have never been so afraid to dance with someone. Slowly, we begin the dance.

It's a funny way, "I say, "the music is so beautiful but more important, I have dreamt of dancing with you for the last six months"

She smiles, "I know."

I want to ask her, How do you know ?' but the question doesn't come to my lips and all I say is 'I never got your name what is it?'

"Kavita,"

'What a lovely name'

"You think so?"

"Yes, It means poetry, "I say and I am wondering whether this beautiful girl can read the fear in my stomach.

"This is going to be a long night." She says.

"Yes it is, but I hope it will be longer and we can dance forever"

"Yes, we can dance till morning, and in between I will make you a sandwich of ham and chicken."

I am wondering if today is my day, is it going to be my conquest, my victory? We dance and now I pull her closer to me.

I say, "I realized that I would rather look at your beauty than I would look at the sunrise. tonight, I overcame the fear."

As we dance, I tell her I am an amateur painter and I have been making her paintings. She is astonished. and says, " I want to see it."

"You will have to come to my apartment"

"Let's go"

"She switches off the record and I gather her in my arms, cradle her enter my apartment, and stand before the painting.

This feels like a dream, and I begin to wonder if paintings can sense anything. But a painting cannot hallucinate, and I cannot dream. This is real, or at least as real as one can call our lives. "It is very beautiful," She says, "you have depicted me so correctly."

"I have been wanting to tell you of your beauty since you came here," I say, fighting the urge to run from her. Maybe it is time to turn and face my fear.

She blushes and takes my hand in hers. She picks up the painting and together we move back to her room. She switches on the record again and places the painting next and says, "How did you make this painting without my dress? You painted me in the nude; Have you been fantasizing about me?"

I do not answer as the music begins. I hold her and dance again. It feels electric as if our hands will catch fire. I meet her eyes, which are filled with love as much as they are with joy.

"Such beauty as yours cannot be matched, but your words mean more to me than I can say," she says. She breaks the steps of the dance and places a kiss on the back of my hand. I gasp, and she pulls away.

"I did not mean to frighten you," I say, "that was just unexpected." I take her free hand in mine and place a gentle kiss on the inside of her wrist.

"I never did catch your name," she says, meeting my gaze.

"It's Kavita and you?

"Raunaq Singh"

We dance together Her hand lands on my waist, a gentle gesture in the dancing world, and a touch that means so much more to me than anyone perceiving it could ever know. I'm getting my confidence back and I move forward and lightly brush her lips. But there is an animal in her, and she responds with her tongue in my mouth.

As I suck her tongue, I say," I wish this could continue forever, and the night would never end."

"I also wish the same"

There is not much of a place in the room and suddenly she catches the stool and she stumbles, but I hold her and now I have carried her in my arms and taken her on the couch.

What a beautiful moment it was. I can't have enough of it. I have now pulled this short skit up and the high-waist panty comes into view.

I put my thumb in the elastic and wrench it up. It's a flimsy piece, decorative and dainty and not meant to stand such pressure, and the same tears at the seam and I throw it away what I have dreamed for six months now comes true as I hide my face at the altar of her beauty.

The entire night was spent in rare transport of joy. Afterward, I can get to my apartment in the morning and once more we are transported to Paradise, I realize I have not had a woman for three years and I can't have enough of her.

We dance the rest of the night our words and our movements matching in grace. When the morning is approaching, we take a rest. I sit down next to her, and she wraps her arm around my shoulders. It is impossible for a painting to get cold, but the gesture is more than enough.

Nirvana

The night sky slowly lightens, and I sit up. I feel my time is running out, and I have something more to say.

"Kavita?" I say,," I want to say something."

"What is it, Raunaq?" She says the name effortlessly, and I am delighted..

"I am in love with you. I have been since you came to the flat," I say, the words easily. I never could have predicted it was so easy to confess to her.

" I also, my dear Raunaq." The first rays of color start to peek over the window, and I sigh.

"Until tomorrow night?" It is not a question I expect her to answer. I lean to kiss and realize her smile is beautiful but sad. For six months, she was the woman across my flat.

There is always a twist to the tail and the twist took place. I say," Wait, I am coming from the washroom." I enter and come out as fast as possible but the beauty is not there and the room is empty I shout 'Where are you' There is no response. I look around for nobody. I open the door and look at the door of the flat in front of me. It's open I enter but there is nobody but somehow I feel happy. Maybe she would find happiness also. I look out of the balcony to the rising sun, and I realize this was one long night that was wonderfully spent. The girl had vanished and realized that I was never going to see her again. Did I feel sad? I can't see, but I can recollect that I felt happy at the moment of love, which had been bestowed on me by God, none other than Lord Krishna.

.

CHAPTER SEVEN

THE COURT MARTIAL

A BIZZARRE TALE

The Court Marshal had assembled, and the judge Advocate looked at the other two members of the Court Marshal, one a captain and the other a Major, and said," We shall start proceedings once the Presiding Officer, Commander Ronak Singh comes." The Commander soon came, a regal man, almost 48, battle-hardened airman, but still a bachelor. He came and sat in the presiding officer's chair and the Judge Advocate(JA) said, "Sir, can we start the proceedings by swearing in the members?"

"Yes, let's start immediately"

The formalities were completed, and Ronak Singh opened the case details folder. He remembered that he had received a telephone call from the Command Judge Advocate (CJA) nominating him to preside over a Court Martial in Jaisalmer. He was instructed to proceed immediately to try an NCO accused of forgery and misappropriation of (Service) property. He had been charged under various offenses of the Indian Penal Code. In addition, Section 65 of the Air Force Act which covers any Act Prejudicial to Good Order and Discipline was also slapped on the accused Ram Singh, an NCO of the Tech trade.

The first day of the court was over once the accused had been arraigned and charged with the offenses. Ronak Singh adjourned the court for two days. He instructed the JA to reconvene the court on Monday as Saturday and Sunday were holidays. He went to his chamber and perused the Court of Inquiry, and the Summary of Evidence and concluded that there was a watertight case against the NCO.

Jaisalmer is a lovely place with sand surrounding the city. With the sun setting, he decided that he would go for a ride. He rang up the NCO in charge of the office and told him that he wanted to go for a ride in the desert sand. The NCO immediately arranged for a horse from the nearby Army cavalry unit. He informed Ronak the horse would be ready in 15 minutes, and could Ronak come to the stables of the Army cavalry unit to take charge of the horse.

Ronak rode out into the desert. The sun was setting and now it was very cool and a soft wind blew. He rode for some time and then far away, he could see a figure standing under a tree. Curiosity got the better of him and he rode towards the tree and the figure under the tree. As he neared, he realized that a small oasis existed in the desert and there were many trees there. He rode to the tree and was foxed when he saw a lovely woman with a low sari standing there. She looked extremely picturesque with the cold wind blowing making her hair dance and adding an aura of mystery to her beauty.

Ronak could make out that she was a very lovely woman. He brought the horse close to her and asked, "Who are you?"

"What does it matter, " she replied

"Yes," he said, "it doesn't frankly"

The woman now spoke, "You are the officer who is the Presiding Officer of the Court-Martial."

Ronak was surprised that the girl knew about this and said, "Yes, I am but how do you know this?"

"I guessed it because I hadn't seen a gentleman ride in a year in the desert for a long time."

The horse was close to the girl who was standing on the dune, making her face almost level with his chin and he looked into her eyes and said, "You are very beautiful but it is very strange that you should be moving around here in the desert when it will be night soon and everything will be dark."

She didn't reply, and he asked her. "What is your name?"

"Guddu."

"what does it mean?"

"It means a doll," she explained.

Something strange happened and by a quirk the horse became restive and it rose on its hind legs and shook wildly. Ronak was caught off balance and clutched the girl while falling to the earth. As he hit the sand he realized the girl was on top of him and wanted to say 'sorry.' He is 48 and his reflexes are a little slow, if such a thing had happened 10 years back, he would have controlled the horse easily.

He lay on the sand with the girl on top of him, and then something strange happened again. The girl began to kiss him. Ronak reciprocated and the soft lips and the tongue of the girl, probing his mouth, overwhelmed him. He began to reciprocate the kiss with all the ardour he had.

"Oh my Lord," the girl whispered, "you are so strong like the warrior Bhima."

"Bhima?" he asked involuntarily.

"Yes, like the time, the great warrior had fertilized 80 virgins."

The girl bit Ronak and egged him forward. She had opened the buttons of her blouse and Ronak was in shock as she was not wearing any bra. Her peaks of desire looked almost virginal, and he involuntarily began to suckle her nipples. He had lost his sense of reason. In the darkening gloom of the desert, he unloosened the cord of her petticoat. She lifted her hips for him to slide it down. He pulled it off her and threw, it away. The clothing fell, some distance away. The wind was beginning to blow fast and the dress was carried away for many hundreds of yards, lost perhaps forever as the swirling sand buried it. At that time, he did not think about it, but later realised that perhaps it was an act of Providence.

He was now witness to her mons, curls, firm thighs, the flat belly, indeed, she was a sight to be witnessed by the gods. The Inevitable happened. They became all mouths and fingers and tongues and senses. Their mouths sought each other, a nipple, a clitoris. They lay entangled, moving very slowly. They kissed until the kissing became torture and the body grew restless. Their hands always found yielding flesh, an opening. The sand they lay on gave off an earthy odour, which mingled with the odours of their bodies. They tried to come in unison, but Guddu came first, falling in a heap, Ronak fell beside her, As Guddu's pleasure grew fainter, rolling away, dying off, Ronak bit into her tender flesh. In the paroxysm of her pleasure, Guddu didn't feel the teeth buried there.

Now he was at the apex and with vigour lunged forward even as she allowed him to enter her siege and the sacred part of her body.

He lay panting on the sand in the darkness, and then he was conscious of the girl beside him. "Did you like it?" she asked.

"Yes"

"Will you do something for me?"

"Anything under the sun."

Then she began to apply her hand to his phallus, and it rose like the Phoenix, the mythical bird as it rose from its ashes.

In between nibbles, she whispered," Tomorrow and the day after are holidays and you can have me any number of times but on Monday you have to acquit Ram Singh."

Finale

The words hit him like a ton of bricks and he began to wonder what would happen next. It was also bizarre, it was like he had eaten the forbidden fruit like Adam, and now he was into a paroxysm of delight and desire. Maybe he would have to pay a price for it.The next two days passed so quickly that Ronak never knew when the sun rose and when it set. He was having a woman after years, and the desire to eat the forbidden fruit was tremendous.

In the middle of the night on Sunday, he had his last bout and marvelled at the exercise of his power over her. For the umpteenth time he suckled her temple leading her and him to the acme of satisfaction.

On Monday, the trial commenced, but Ronak was not the same man who had sat in the Presiding officer's chair on Friday. Here was a different man smitten by something so lovely that all he craved for was a world of flesh.

It was the end of the District Court Marshal and the accused was brought and the JA asked Ronak and other members of the court whether they had concluded.

"Yes", Ronak replied, "we have and I will read out the verdict." He had made up his mind and very softly said, that the evidence was not substantive to convict the man and all charges against him be dismissed. The JA was surprised and he said," But sir, the evidence is conclusive, how can you make this decision?"

"I don't think so," Ronak replied, and much later when the accused was brought before the court, the JA announced the verdict that the man had been acquitted of all charges.

In the judgment, he wrote that the NCO must immediately be posted to a forward area and serve time on active duty.

Ram Singh bowed his head to the presiding officer even as he exulted at the verdict. Things now began to move at great speed and Ram Singh was on his way to Ladakh.

It was evening and once again, Ronak mounted the horse and rode out into the desert. He was hoping he would see the girl again but as much as he moved around, he could not locate anybody and he came back to the mess The next day he took the flight back to his unit, but the enduring image of Guddu and her possession by him flashed again and again before his mind.

A month later he was just sitting in his living room and the orderly brought a sheet of files for him to peruse. He opened the first one and found a message from the headquarters informing him that one soldier named Ram Singh had been killed in a border clash in the Galvan Valley. He immediately got up and picked up the telephone to get confirmation of the news.

There was no doubt that it was the same man he had acquitted in the court, and now God had dispensed justice and he had gone to the land of Hades.

He had made up his mind and immediately typed out his resignation letter emailed it and left for Jaisalmer. He reached the camp station, and once again asked for the horse and rode out into the desert. He had an uncanny feeling that what had happened had to happen and the door to paradise had opened for him. As he rode far away to the same tree under the oasis, he observed a woman standing. He knew it was her and he galloped towards the figure. He reached it and soon realized that it was Guddu. She looked at Ronak with a quizzical look.

He rode up to her and within a moment, gathered her in his arms, and positioned her in the saddle in front of him

"What are you doing? "She asked.

"Something which God has asked me to do."

He pressed the spurs, and the horse began to gallop forward. It was a furious gallop through the sand. He held the girl in his arms and pushed her forward. The skirt had already risen to her waist, he pushed her forward, and lo and behold he commenced the primordial act with her on the horse. It was a swift movement and he was sheathed inside her.

"No,", she said, "no, you have sent my man to death. If you had not acquitted him, he would have gone only to jail but now he is no more." Ronak was in no mood for anything and even as the horse moved forward he had possessed her completely. The movement of the horse as it galloped furiously in the sand added impetus to the exotic union.

The horse now stopped, and with Guddu in his arms, he slipped to the soft sand and whispered to her," My love. I have come back."

Ronak was in for a surprise because the girl slapped him and ran away.

Well, folks, that is the end of the story. What happened next? did Ronak get his girl after all? Did she realize that what had happened was only because the Lord had willed it? After all Lord Krishna has said that *'not a leaf moves without my will on this earth.'*

But that's another story for another day and I will close now and say that sometimes the truth can be stranger than fiction.

CHAPTER EIGHT

TALE FROM THE JUNGLE

Don Wilson was a well-known, senior manager of a tea plantation near the Indian city of Jorhat. The vast plantations of this area are a gift of the British Raj and in the period the story is written, that is the 1930s, the Raj was the only portent power in India. Don Wilson was enjoying his books and perquisites as part of the ruling elite in India. He was born in India and travelled only once to England and it has for him a terrible time. He never wished to go there again. It was the winter that disturbed him, the cold and overcast skies and now and then blowing air into the fire hearth was not his cup of tea. He didn't like it at all and he was glad he came back to India. He has resided in Assam for nearly 40 years and for the last 20 years has been part of the Stanley Dockyard tea plantation. Wilson was a bachelor, which is something other people couldn't understand. He was handsome and strong. A big game Shikari was a man who had shot a tiger at close quarters, yet he was single and alone in the lonely plantation. Don Wilson had a problem and he could not discuss it with anybody. All the people he met, never knew that inside Wilson was consumed by a fear of the unknown. Whenever he approached a woman he would panic and his seed would flow out and he was left, wondering what had happened. He had tried it a few times but now, he had decided that he would maintain his macho Image, but not cohabit with another woman.

He was sitting in his bungalow spread over an acre of land, when one of the Nepali boys came up to him and said, " Hazur, there is some fear among the people."

Don Wilson had endeared himself to the people and employees of the plantation. Vicariously, he liked them. He asked the boy what had happened. The boy replied sombrely, "Sir, in the temple of the Goddess Kali, people have seen a nude woman dancing. "Don Wilson was all alert now. "Come, my man," he said," all this is mumbo-jumbo. How can anybody be dancing in the Temple?"

"Yes sir, it is true"

"I don't believe it, such things happen only in fairy tales. Maybe somebody is creating a myth."

"No sir, I suggest you go and see what is happening"

Don Wilson went inside opened the big black cupboard and took out his rifle. It was the one gifted to him by his grandfather, Karl Wilson, and he had used it in the 1879 war against the Afghans in the battle of Kandahar".

This was the same rifle that he had used to kill the tiger who had turned maneater. The beast was just 10 feet away from him. He remembered the tiger looking at him with his eyes burning like coal embers in the night. It was pitch dark, there was stillness all around, maybe the jungle had realized the king of beasts had come. The tiger had looked at Wilson and snarled. It was a signal that he wanted a battle. Things had happened in a flurry. The tiger had jumped. Don Wilson had pulled the trigger, the sound of the gun firing reverberated through the jungle, but Don Wilson was no mean shot and the bullet had hit the beast between the eyes. The tiger had leaped towards Don Wilson, but once the bullet entered him, he seemed to crumble, and as he reached Don Wilson, he was almost dead. Wilson fired twice more, and the tiger hit him and rolled to one side, even as Wilson fell to the ground. It was now all over bar the shouting because the tiger was dead and suddenly there was a lot of bustle all around and Nepali boys and labourers were running here and there and they came up and said sir you have killed the tiger.

Wilson remembered the incident lifted his rifle and said," I will go to the Kali Temple and see who this dancer is."

The boy looked at Don Wilson, and said," Sir, nobody else will go with you."

Wilson smiled, and said," Don't worry my man I will go there alone."

Don Wilson, once again smiled. He picked up his gun and cocked the weapon and said, "I will go alone my friend but what happened to the priest, is he there?"

"Sir, the priest has run away."

"Ha, I had expected it. I think you people are a superstitious lot but don't worry I will go and check who this person is."

The man walked to his jeep. This was the vehicle that he used in the jungle. He sat in the vehicle and placed the rifle by his side, pressed the ignition, and the engine started. He was glad that Aman Gurang had cleaned the vehicle and made it spick and span and as he put the vehicle into gear it moved forward and soon he was off into the jungle.

He drove very slowly because the road was uneven and soon he had left his estate and moved through the beautifully cropped tea gardens. A cool breeze blew and Don felt extremely happy but at the same time, he had misgivings. He wondered who this dancer was. Was it a ghost or illusion or a real woman? He planned to find out soon.

The power

He reached the Kali Temple on the outskirts of the jungle got out from the jeep and looked at the temple whose silhouette stood out in the darkness. Nobody was there, making him wonder how he had been so foolish as to believe the boy. In such a desolate place, there could not be anybody. He began to walk to the temple through the thick foliage and reached the gate. All around there was darkness and he could not see anything, and then he heard a silvery laugh.

Don Wilson's heartbeat was fast, but he felt no fear because the laugh was of a young girl, but he feared meeting the girl for a different reason because of his inadequacy. He wanted to go away now. He was sure that some living person had come into the temple posing as a supernatural dancer, all he said was, "Who is there?"

There was no reply, and after some time, he was thinking of going away. He took out his torch and switched on the powerful beam. The torch lit up the temple and he went into the temple. He held the torch in one hand and the rifle in the other. After a moment he thought, what the hell! why should I carry this rifle with me, after all the person here is only a girl.

He placed the rifle against the wall of the temple and then looked around the small crypt. The image of the Goddess Kali showed up in the light from the torch. He looked at the icon and had an uncanny feeling that the statute was alive. A moment later, he dismissed the thought as a figment of his imagination, an illusion.

He thought for a moment and then decided to move closer to the statue of the goddess. As he neared the statue, he unmistakably heard the laughter of a girl again now the heartbeats of Don Wilson quickened, and the adrenalin rushed to his brain. He wanted to find out what was happening. He swung the torch around the small prayer hall, but they were nobody, except him and the statue of the Goddess Kali.

And then something strange happened, just a distance away, he could make out the figure of a young woman moving towards him from the door. The light from the torch lit up her face and body. Don Wilson was in for a shock. The torch almost fell from his hands, as he observed that the woman slowly moving towards him was nude. His eyes riveted on her mons, and he could see this abundance of curls crowning her temple.

The more he looked at the girl, the more he liked her. She could not have been more than 18 or 19, and considering that Wilson was over 40, he realized the tremendous age difference.

"Who are you?" He asked.

They were no reply, except, he could make out from the light of the torch that girl was smiling. She said nothing but again laughed. Now he could see her body. He could make out a lovely sculptured face, large oval-shaped eyes, black hair long and enticing, a slender neck, sloping shoulders, and the crowning bust line, so firm and erect. Wilson felt a stirring in his lions, but at the same time, he was also overtaken by panic. Now the girl had moved closer to him and he could make out more clearly the black curls on her mons and the flat belly. He could observe that the naval housed a massive diamond. Oh God, he thought who is this and how could this person come here?

The Englishman repeated the question, "Who are you?"

"The Goddess Kali has sent me to help you"

"Help me, what the hell are you talking about? How can you help me?"

"I am going to help you to become a man again"

Wilson was silent for a moment, wondering what was happening, and momentarily shut his eyes, and when he opened them, he was in for a shock. He found that he was standing by a small throne and many people were around. In front of him was the girl he had just seen in the temple.

"Huzur," the girl said, "please sit on the throne I am going to dance for you."

Don Wilder was wondering what was happening but he sat on the throne. He realized that he was wearing the attire of an Indian king, and now the girl began to do the Bharatanatyam dance before him. She lifts her hands and bangs her foot down, and she is ravishing. His eyes all the time riveted on her mons. The dance continued, and somebody was playing a drum and the girl in classical Bharatnatyam style was lifting her foot and banging it down and when she lifted her book, her leg Wilson's eyes caught a glimpse of the treasure beneath the curls. Oh God, he thought what's happening to me?

The dance continued for some time and then the girl came to him, and said, "My Lord come with me."

Don Wilson was in a panic. He didn't want to go with her, and he knew his inadequacy, but then she held his hands and slowly led him out of the hall, and into an adjacent chamber with a luxurious bed. She made him sit on the bed and began to kiss him.

"Don't panic," she said.

Wilson whispered, "Stop it. Please stop all this."

"No," she replied, "the goddess has sent me, and I obey her."

She had now complete control over Wilson. He lay on the bed but wanted to run away. His legs were powerless, even as the girl took his manhood in her mouth.

That was the key moment, and Don Wilson thought he was going to lose, but he steeled himself, because very soon, the tension began to go from his body, and he became strong.

Through his eyes, he could watch the beautiful girl hover over him. They were no doubt she was something rare and beautiful, the like of which he had never seen; so fair and white with pink lips, and large eyes, but once again, his eyes again and again riveted on her body and he sighed in relief as tension left his body.

The girl now lying on the bed whispered, "Become the tiger"

"No," Wilson, whispered," no, it is not possible"

"Try"

Don Wilson got up, he was witness to the exotic sight of the girl pulling her legs, and at the same time held him as she directed him to the Citadel.

Don Wilson closed his eyes and allowed the girl to lead him forward. He felt the panic going away from him. Even as he thrust inside her, he gave a primal cry of victory, and he knew he was going to win.

He felt like he was floating on the clouds with the stars all around, and he was at peace, almost like reaching Nirvana.

As he fell on the girl, suckling her nipples, he closed his eyes. A clash of thunder and lightning flashed across the sky, and when Don opened his eyes, he saw he was lying on the floor. They were nobody there except him, but he was naked, and he was wondering where his clothes were. He looked around. There was nobody, and he wondered what had happened. Was it a dream or a real act? he arose, dressed, came out, and went to his bungalow.

He reached the bedroom and fell asleep. He had no time to think about what happened. Was it an apparition, a reality or what was it? He woke up the next morning and there was a crowd all around. A few people came to him and asked, "Have you been to the temple and have you seen that there is a dancer there."

He was quiet for a moment and said," Yes I've been there, but there is nobody there and I can tell you friends you can go there now and there is nobody." He had a new confidence and he remembered that when he had thrust into that beautiful girl, she had whispered, "The Goddess Kali has made you into a man now, go and take as many women as you want; you deserve it because you have looked after the people so well that the Goddess is pleased, I will go now as my job is done."

The mystery

A few days elapsed, and, he asked a few of the tea garden employees If they had seen any dancing girl and everybody said no, we had not seen anybody at all, but Don Wilson knew better. He knew he had met an apsara sent by the goddess. He looked around, with a new confidence, and espied a young girl standing nearby. He had looked at her and was in shock. There was no doubt that it was the same girl whom he had met in the temple. He wondered how he could correlate the events, the girl in the temple and the girl, standing here; what had happened? he had no explanation.

This is the story of Don Wilson, who was made into a man again by the goddess Kali what did Don Wilson do

? he became a devotee of the goddess and still wonders how the transformation took place. Well, it's something like Ripley's Believe it or Not. But what I write is an absolute fact. So farewell friends, enjoy the story and relate it to your children, and tell them that the goddess Kali manifests in many ways to help humans who do good. But what about the girl? well, she lived with Don Wilson and bore him many children.

CHAPTER NINE

THE SPY

The beginning

This is a story almost 50 years old and was related to me by a senior officer who was my mentor. He was an Air Marshal, and he sat in the bar with us over a glass of scotch and told us this tale. The background was the 1971 war with Pakistan and the setting was the city of Agra. The city is famous for the Taj Mahal and for an important Air Force strike base. This base housed in those days the Canberra Mark II medium bomber and was the strike base of the Central Air Command. The Pakistan Air Force launched the attack on 3 December 1971, In a pre-emptive strike, but much before that they had a meeting in Rawalpindi. The meeting decided that they needed a spy who would go to Agra. This was many months before the war commenced.

The man selected was a corporal of the Pakistani Air Force; a very intelligent young man who had volunteered to go. He was given the names of a few other Muslim persons residing in Agra who would help him. The major had said matter-of-factly." almost 15% of the Indian population professes the Muslim faith, and these people are not exactly loyal to the country."

All arrangements were made for the corporal whose name was Aftab and he was given a new identity with a Hindu name and an air ticket to go to Kathmandu. From there, he took a bus, crossed the Indian border, and reached Agra. On reaching Agra he immediately got in touch with one of the people whose address had been given to him. He knocked on the door of the house and it was opened by a lady. She asked," Who are you?"

He replied," You must have got a message. I have come from Pindi but for now, my name will be Bhima Singh, though my name is Altaf."

The lady quickly took the man inside and said, "It's good you have come, but we must be careful. You will have to recon the entire area and your main purpose will be to keep an eye on the Air Force. The rest is up to you. You must have been briefed by the headquarters."

The war was still a month away and Altaf got down to the task of reconnoitring the Airfield. He would spend hours moving around the airfield and with his camera taking photographs by climbing up the tree from where he could see the airfield and, in the distance, the parked bombers. After some time, he began to feel lonely, and he needed the company of a woman.

He was wondering what to do, and he thought that the Inmates of the house would give him one of the women to cohabitate with, but they did not seem interested and kept him at arm's length. His frustration grew and he finally, one day went to the market. He entered a grocery shop and saw a young girl buying some vegetables. The young girl in a Salwar kameez also noticed Altaf. He was a handsome man. Being a Punjabi, he was fair and had a muscular body and deep blue eyes. The girl saw him. She hadn't seen him before and she wondered who he was, her mind in some confusion. Her bag was open and the vegetables she had bought fell on earth. Altaf immediately got up and picked up the vegetables. He helped place the vegetables back and said softly," You must be more careful but when you go home, please wash the vegetables thoroughly before you can resume them."

The girl saw Altaf and smiled, and she couldn't help feeling that he had a very infectious smile. She did not know that this man was a spy sent by the Pakistan Air Force to keep an eye on the Agra Air Force base.

The next step

Altaf saw the girl walk away, but he was smitten by her, and he was wondering what to do. He decided to follow the girl. He kept a safe distance and followed the girl. She had left the market and Altaf realized that she had come to the red-light area, his heartbeat quick as he realized that possibly the girl was a prostitute, but there was no denying the fact that she was very beautiful and he began to wonder about her beauty. He kept looking at the house. As she entered, he made a mental note of it and then went back. The next day he again went to the same shop and waited for a long time. After some time, he observed the girl come again, and when she saw Altaf her smile brightened. She said," It's so nice to see you here again."

"I've been waiting for you."

"Really?"

"Yes"

"Oh my," she said, "you don't know a thing about me, by the way, what is your name ?" He says, "My name is Bhima

Singh and I have come from Rohtak in Haryana."

The girl just smiled at him and said, "Bhima Singh. Why don't you come and meet me in my house?"

It was an invitation he was not going to refuse. He said," Yes, I will come, but you must give me the address." He of course knew where she stayed. The girl gave him the address and he smiled at her and she smiled back at him and left. He watched the receding figure and realized how beautiful she was with an extremely well-shaped back, a small waist, and a beautiful bust. Altaf was feeling very lonely, and he went home, and the entire family sat down to dinner and they asked Altaf "What the hell is going on man, why are you so silent?"

"I'm feeling lonely."

"You are selected to do a job," one of the men said, "but at the same time, I must assure you that we will help you but have control over yourself because if anybody comes to know that you are a Pakistani spy you can get into serious trouble. Not only that, but you will also drag us into the hands of the authorities."

Altaf remembered this meeting, but he had made up his mind to gratify himself because he liked the girl, he had seen at the grocery shop.

After a few days, Altaf made his way to the house where he had seen the girl enter. In the meantime, war clouds were gathering and the battle in East Pakistan had commenced. The Indian Army had moved into East Pakistan in a big way and was being helped by the Mukti Bahani. The battle was going badly for the Pakistan Army in the east. General Headquarters in Rawalpindi had decided that they would have to do something else to restore the balance. They decided that Pakistan must attack Indian air bases as quickly as possible and one of the Air Marshalls commented that it would be like the Israeli strike on Egypt in 1967 when 90% of the Egyptian air force had been destroyed on the ground.

Before leaving, Altaf had been given a small transmitter and he had been told to only use it in an emergency. He was also told that if required he would be contacted. At the same time, he was warned to switch it off so that nobody could detect any signal. On 2 December, when he was sitting in his room, the transmitter came alive, and a voice came to the line. "Is it you?"

"yes sir," Altaf asked.

"Yes, tomorrow is the day we are going to move forward in a pre-emptive strike on seven Indian airfields and decimate all of them. You must reach the Airfield tomorrow and see the effect of our bombing so that you can take photos and tell us the effect of the attack. After that immediately leave Agra and come back."

"Yes sir, "Altaf replied.

He felt happy, and he really wanted to go back but before that, he wanted to meet that beautiful girl again, and he quickly got up, and in the twilight began to walk towards the red-light area.

It didn't take him long to reach the place. He knocked on the door of the house. There was a strange quietness all around and soon the door opened and lo and behold he was witness to his lady love, whom he had met at the grocery shop.

She opened the door allowed Altaf to enter, and said," Bhima, it's nice you have come, but do you know what sort of job I do?"

"Yes, I know, and I don't hold it against you but please take me in your arms. I will give you any amount of money you want."

The girl smiled and said, "Come with me to the attic up, that is a place where we will not be disturbed." They went to the small attic which had a bed, and a dim light was burning. The girl looked at Altaf and said, "It will cost you ₹500, now take off your clothes and after that, I will show myself to you." Altaf removed his trousers and then the girl was in for a shock because she saw that Altaf's sex had been circumcised. She was in a bit of a quandary because he had told her his name was Bhima Singh, yet it was clear he was not a Hindu because if he was a Hindu, he would not be circumcised. Her mind was in a whirl. Why should this man tell her a lie? Could he be a spy who has come from God knows where?"

She had serviced Muslim clients before, but none of them had claimed to be a Hindu, and the fact that this man had claimed to be a Hindu had aroused her suspicion

She looked at Altaf and said, "You wait here for a few minutes, I will bring a small bottle of whiskey from the shop downstairs. We will first drink it and then you can have me to your heart's content."

Altaf felt very confident, but before she left, he kissed her eyes and lips. The girl left, but she did not go to the liquor shop immediately but to the small telephone booth nearby. She quickly dialled the number of the police, and a man came online. Everybody was alert because war clouds were hovering over the subcontinent, hence, the response was immediate.

A man asked, "What is it?"

"Sir" the girl replied, "I think in my room there is a Pakistani spy."

"Are you sure?"

"Almost, but you better send somebody to check up on this."

"Don't worry, I'm passing a message immediately to the military intelligence and they will be there very soon, give your location."

"How much time you will take?"

"Not more than 15 minutes"

She looked at her watch and, slowly, went to the liquor shop. She wanted to pass away as much time as possible. She picked up a bottle of Black Knight whiskey paid ₹ 600 for it, and carrying it in her bag, began to walk back to her apartment. Her heart beat fast for all of a sudden she was a patriot and she wasn't going to betray the country if this man was a Pakistani spy that was a big scoop. She was more than certain that he was a Muslim and perhaps a spy because Hindus do not get circumcision done.

She walked very slowly, to kill as much time as possible. She was waiting for 15 minutes to elapse. The 15 minutes passed and then far away, she saw a brown jeep coming, which stopped outside the house. She had also reached the door of the house, and in the jeep had a captain, and two men armed with automatic rifles. No words were spoken as she began to lead the men up to the attic.

Altaf was sitting on the bed and his excitement was increasing by the moment There was a knock on the door and the girl entered. She was indeed very lovely and then that girl asked him," You said your name was Bhim Singh but how is it that you are circumcised?"

The question hit Altaf like a sledgehammer and he couldn't answer, and at that moment he knew that he had committed a tremendous blunder. "Listen," he said I will confess to you. Yes, I am a Muslim, but I love you."

"But what are you doing here? Have you come from Pakistan?"

Altaf just looked at her with a straight intent gaze. "If I tell you the truth, will you still let me sleep with you?" The girl looked at the Altaf, but patriotism overtook her, and she kept silent. The door opened and in a moment two guards with a submachine gun entered along with the captain. Altaf was caught.

"Pull up your trousers man," the captain said, "we are going to take you to the interrogation centre."

Altaf looked at the girl and said," Whoever you are. I liked you from the very first day you came to the grocery shop. I thought I would spend happy moments with you, but you have betrayed me."

The girl looked straight at Altaf and said, "I'm sorry but 2 and 2 don't add up. You gave me a Hindu name and you turned out to be circumcised. You were hiding the fact that you are a Muslim, and that is a very dangerous thing."

the-girl-and-the-

spy

End

The men took Altaf away and nobody knows what happened to him. The girl now sat on the bed and began to wonder, whether she had done the right thing. She closed her eyes and prayed and asked God to give her strength. Altaf had spilled the beans to his interrogators and the AOC commanding Agra had dispersed the bombers. So, when the strike took place, the result was a big zero. The Air Marshall looked at me and said," Hi Capt., I hope you like the tale?"

"yes" I replied," but what happened to the girl; did she get anything?

The air marshal just scratched his head and said, "I frankly don't know but, in those days, there was a patriotic fervor all around and even the prostitutes wanted to do their bit for the country. A sense of patriotism overrode e

CHAPTER TEN

HAMLETS UNFINISHED TALE

Some tales are difficult to relate, and this story comes in the same genre. I remember as a young captain, I had proceeded to France for a conversion course on the Mirage IV. We started off with the theory classes as a first step. As in college, I was always one of the backbenchers and I did the same thing in this class and occupied the last seat. I had already one companion in the last row and it turned out to be a beautiful French girl with golden hair, obviously, she was also going to get converted onto the new plane, after the class was over, I decided I must get myself introduced to this muse I walked up to her in the coffee shop and introduced myself. It was a Wonderful introduction, and we shook hands and decided to have a 2nd cup of coffee together.

During the coffee, we got into an animated conversation, and suddenly the girl whose name is Winnie asked me. What are you doing in the evening today?

Nothing much replied

Well, would you like to come to watch a play of Shakespeare?

Now Shakespeare is a man who I admire a lot, and I can say without compunction that I have watched most his plays enacted on the stage and read each of them in a book titled 'collected Works of William Shakespeare", which was presented to be my father on one of my birthdays.

"Which is the play being staged today?," I asked.

Her eyes brightened, and she said," it is 'hamlet.' I love his character."

" Fine," I replied, " how about you picking me up from the officers mess where I'm staying?"

The evening went like clockwork mechanism. I in particular enjoyed, the play which was staged by a troupe from London. After the play was over, we sat down and kept area and had a hamburger and coffee and discussed the play. After finishing our meal, I suggested that she could drop me back to the mess. She mentioned that the guardroom would be closed and entry would not be allowed inside as it was pretty late, and then spontaneously suggested that I could come over to a place and spend the night there.. I looked at the girl and decided this was a good proposition and after watching such a wonderful place, it would be a good idea to discuss something more about Shakespeare with her in our house.

We reach apartment and she asked me inside and then told me to sit down on the couch and she would come soon. Where are you going? Asked she replied that she was going to change into something more comfortable and she would bring a set of clothes for me as well..

After about 15 minutes, I heard a sound and I was really taken back to see a warrior approaching me dressed in the same dress and armour of omelette. I knew she was my host and I was wondering what she was doing in this outlandish out.

What are you wearing? I asked.

I am wearing the armour, which hamlet wear, and I have a sword in my hand

I just smiled. That's it. It's a wonderful. Wait. Welcome me, and you look good in the armour and the sword, but what does it signify?

She replied, this signifies that hammer has come inside me now, and he is testing for plant, just like he was thirsting for the flat office stepfather

And being a little silly, I asked

Now she replied, and she pointed to the wall and said there is a pointer there. Please take it because you will have to give that to me.

I don't take it seriously. I said okay if you want to play a game, I don't mind it.

I walked up to the ball and saw the pointer hanging there and took it and held it in my hand, and now the girl began to move towards me a little awkward because she was wearing an armour

Aashiqui closer, I could make out the deadly intent in her eyes, and I was a little under. I was wondering if the girl was normal, listen, I said," what the hell are you doing?"

"I am playing the role of Hamlet."

"That's fine, but why? and with whom are you going to battle?"

"I'm going to battle with you."

I felt a tingling at the back of my neck and spine, and realise that I was going to be in some serious problem, If I didn't think about something quickly. I thought I would frighten the girl and I swished my sword up and down. She saw me flourish the sword, but instead of frightening her, it spurred her into action. She looked at me and said softly," Why, you can handle the sword, well, you remind me of Laertius, the brother of the girl Hamlet loved. I love Hamlet."

"That means you're making me into a villain"

"Yes, very true"

The girl now stood before me with her sword and aimed a blow, I parried it. I looked into her eyes and saw nothing but deadly intent. She was breathing heavily and said, "you better watch out because I am going to kill you."

"Are you crazy?" I said, 'you can't do such things."

She just laughed. What is going to happen is going to be decided later, but right now you defend yourself and again she swished her sword to strike me a blow. The blow soon came and I parried it with my sword. I was thinking what to do, and then realised that

she was a woman, and I could very well, be the victor if I used my superior strength, considering the fact I was of the top boxer of my squadron. I decided the best thing was to confuse her. I looked at her and said almost in a whisper for heightened effect," There is someone behind you." This simple ploy worked. She looked back and seizing the moment, I was on top of her, and with a mighty swing, snatched the sword from her and sent her scrawling back. As she fell back the helmet hit the sofa, and it appeared to be not very good material because it fell of her head, revealing her golden hair, and now she was only in the armour without a sword, and I was on top of her.

She was taken back and said," you are very strong." I just smiled and didn't see anything, but my being on top of the girl is affecting me in a different manner.

Lying on top of her, I began to unzip what she was wearing, and soon I had thrown it away, Under the protective armour she was wore only lingerie. I think she was stupid and what had happened had sapped her resistance. The fall had also jarred her, and she didn't know what's happening at that moment and what my next move would be. I followed up by removing the flimsy panty, and could see her pert raisings covered with a brief. I put my hand in the elastic and pulled it up. The flimsy lace and elastic, could not stand the pressure of my strength and parted at the seam, and the girl was naked. She looked bewildered and I thought to press home my advantage. After a moment, she blurted, "you haven't played fair and square,"

"Yes," I replied, " but remember all is fair in love and war and this is war." She was silent for a moment, and I continued," I'm going to do something else"

"What are you going to do?"

I did not answer as I began to go kiss her and the ferociousness of the tiger in heat overtook me and by 1 o'clock in the night, I had made her my own.

As we lay panting, I fondled her hair and asked, "what made you do all these things like wearing the helmet and armour, and acting like Hamler and putting my life in danger."

"Oh, I was not going to do anything, I have tried a few other people and all of them, I beat thoroughly and then threw them out of the house. I always wanted to give myself to a man who could prove himself to be stronger than me and today you have won me."

I lifted up and carried her to the bed for an encore

The next day we went back to the classes together, and I was wondering about the night, where the girl dressed as hamlet, had created the unbelievable incident.

I might tell that we had no more encounter of this sort and very soon. I was on my flight back to the home country. I reached home. I had a look at my mobile and found that there was an SMS message. It read, 'It was wonderful the way you fought, I will remember it for a long time.'

I smiled and forgot all about it and soon another two months collapsed and when I was sitting in the morning room, the flight commander came to me and said look captain. He said there is repeated call coming to the crew room asking for you.

I walk to the telephone and took the call, wondering what was the problem and then realise in the room, the mobile phone was not catching the signals. I was surprised that it was the French girl and she said I understood you were in the crew room, but the same time please just go out to the room with the Mobile. I have sent you a message and if you feel inclined, you can act on it.

I went out of the room with my mobile and switched on and found the message it read ,'my warrior. You are the real hamlet and you have beaten me at the same time. You did something which is way of God. You see this in me and should you desire to be a partner with me, I suggest you come pronto to me.' What did it mean? For the record I never went back. This was Hamlets unfinished tale.

CHAPTER ELEVEN

DREAMS DIE

I arrived in my suite in the Club guest house and rang up First Gupta the secretary. He came online and said," Good morning. Who is that?" I reciprocated and after wishing him and telling him my name continued, "I'm back from

Mumbai." "That's nice," he replied," You have been away for about 4 months."

" Yes, you're right, almost 4 months but now I want to relax for a few days."

"Wonderful," he replied, "but in the evening come over for a small get-together that is organized in the Annexe."

"Where is it?"

"Just adjacent to the Maneckshaw Hall? Friend, turn up in Mufti"

"Okay," I replied, "nice to get the invite, I'll be there."

The evening came, and I walked into the Annexe to the Manackshaw Hall and found I was just about 10 minutes late and as per protocol, all the other officers had turned up with their better halves. I looked around and in a corner,

I saw a girl, my heartbeat quickened as I realized she was the same one I had given a lift in my SUV a couple of months back while driving to Mumbai. I was driving alone and Gupta had asked me to take her with me and drop her at her residence in Mulund if possible. I had agreed and I assumed it was the end of the matter. I had forgotten about the incident. But now I remembered, and when I saw the girl the adrenal rushed to my brain.

I waited for some time and then discreetly walked to the girl. I knew her name was Sapna. Even as I walked, I wanted to get away from the party but Col Gupta came across to me and said," Welcome Capt., nice that you turned up, and by the way do you remember that last time while going to Mumbai?"

"Yes," I replied," what of it?"

"Well, come with me" he whispered almost like a conspirator, leading me to the slim girl I had seen a distance away. He led me to her and grandly announced," Hello, here is the man who took you to Mumbai; luckily he just arrived here and I thought I'd call him for the party."

She looked at me, and her face became ashen for a moment, but for a moment only, and brightened up as she turned and replied," It's so nice that you came. I can never forget the journey which I had with you." I nodded and said," Yes, same for me." Even when I uttered these words the images flashed before my eyes of the girl naked, with a storm brewing outside, the window curtains had been pulled aside, and outside, the flashes of lightning could be seen. In the flashes, I could see the brownish patch just below the belly, and then I gasped and remembered saying," My God."

A soft voice had emanated to me as she had said, "You are more like Zeus." At that time I could not understand what she meant. Later, I realized that in between intermittent lightning flashes my phallus was visible to her and the sight may have captivated her. Did she feel like Semele, when she saw Zeus in his glory in a flash of light?

The images went away and I was back to reality. She was smiling. Why? She held out her hand and said, "Come with me" . She led me to the porch just outside. It was winter and very cold. She wore a long coat and she quickly buttoned and held it open and whispered, "Times have changed, and so have I" I looked at her slightly protruding belly, and I knew she was with child. She smiled again and said, "It's yours."

My legs felt weak. This was something for which I was not prepared. I was wondering what I should do but I was tongue-tied. It was dark and a drizzle began. I involuntarily took a step forward and all I could do was to caress the slightly protruding belly. How does it feel for a man to be told that this thing has happened? it was after four months and I asked which month is it. I am in the third month she said.

I went on my knees gently lifted the skirt and kissed the slight bulge. She didn't resist and only said this should remain a secret between us. Nobody will know that she and I had made love in the Taj Hotel in Nasik. I said yes but then the next day we went to the lake also.

"Yes," she replied," I remember what a lovely lake. It was so desolate and there was nobody around and it was the monsoon time and that was great fun."

I remember stripping completely nude. She continued standing and then she followed me. She was nude and I could admire her lithe body and flat belly. She followed me into the water and we were soon in waist-deep water It was so chilly and I remember taking her out of the water and carrying her under a tree. What happened under the tree? I think that was the time when Lord Krishna created life in her belly.

I got up and let her skirt fall and then gathered her in my arms. Is there a future I asked. "No," she said, "there is none because right now I'm going to leave the party and go away."

My heart was now beating fast and I had a feeling that it was going to burst out from my breast. Maybe all this was because I was touching 50 and the girl was a good two decades younger.

I wanted to say wait don't go but the words would not come out of my throat. I was mouthing the words but the voice would not come out of my throat. It was as if a paralysis had overtaken my throat and I had lost the power of speech.

She wanted to go away, but then my legs which had been rubbery suddenly became a lot firmer and I launched myself forward and pulled her to me. There was heavy rain all around and thunder was flashing in the sky. "What are you doing?" She whispered.

I didn't say a word as my lips imprisoned her and my tongue forced itself inside her mouth. I was strong, pretty strong. The porch on which we were standing was dark and now lightning was flashing across the sky and a little distance away I could see the lights of the party which was in full swing.

She pushed me away with the words, "I have to go. Your gift must remain secret."

She looked at me with her mouth open and her dark eyes. I laughed and grabbed her head but this time when I touched her something happened in me which made this touch different from any touch earlier in Nasik or the lake.

She did not resist but lay where I had pulled her, against my chest. And I realized that my heart was beating wildly and that Sapna was trembling against me and the darkness lit by flashes of lightning added its aura to the evening.

I started to kiss her and Sapna raised her head as I lowered mine and we kissed. We had our arms around each other. It was like holding some rare, doomed, extinct bird that I had found. I was very frightened; I am not sure but probably she was frightened too, and we shut our eyes. Nothing happened further, and so she untwined herself from me and moved toward the lighted doors, and entered inside the hall. There was a crash of thunder, and I slowly began to move to the lighted doors.

I entered inside and could not see my girl. Probably she had left and then I realized I had seen her for the last time and I was not going to see her again.

CHAPTER TWELVE

UNREQUITED LOVE

I arrived in my suite in the Club guesthouse and rang up Gupta the secretary. He came online and said," Good morning. Who is that?" I reciprocated and after wishing him and telling him my name continued, "I'm back from Mumbai." "That's nice," he replied," You have been away for about 4 months."

"Yes, you're right, almost 4 months but now I want to relax for a few days."

"Wonderful," he replied, "but in the evening come over for a small get-together that is organized in the Annexe."

"Where is it?"

"Just adjacent to the Maneckshaw Hall? Friend, turn up in Mufti"

"Okay," I replied, "nice to get the invite, I'll be there."

The evening came, and I walked into the Annexe to the Manackshaw Hall and found I was just about 10 minutes late and as per protocol, all the other officers had turned up with their better halves. I looked around and in a corner, I saw a girl, my heartbeat quickened as I realized she was the same one I had given a lift in my SUV a couple of months back while driving to Mumbai. I was driving alone and Gupta had asked me to take her with me and drop her at her residence in Mulund if possible. I had agreed and I assumed it was the end of the matter. I had forgotten about the incident. But now I remembered, and when I saw the girl the adrenal rushed to my brain.

I waited for some time and then discreetly walked to the girl. I knew her name was Sapna. Even as I walked, I wanted to get away from the party but Col Gupta came across to me and said," Welcome Capt., nice that you turned up, and by the way do you remember that last time while going to Mumbai?"

"Yes," I replied," what of it?"

"Well, come with me" he whispered almost like a conspirator, leading me to the slim girl I had seen a distance away. He led me to her and grandly announced," Hello, here is the man who took you to Mumbai; luckily he just arrived here and I thought I'd call him for the party."

She looked at me, and her face became ashen for a moment, but for a moment only, and brightened up as she turned and replied," It's so nice that you came. I can never forget the journey which I had with you." I nodded and said," Yes, same for me." Even when I uttered these words the images flashed before my eyes of the girl naked, with a storm brewing outside, the window curtains had been pulled aside, and outside, the flashes of lightning could be seen. In the flashes, I could see the brownish patch just below the belly, and then I gasped and remembered saying," My God."

Unfulfilled love

A soft voice had emanated to me as she had said, "You are more like Zeus." At that time I could not understand what she meant. Later, I realized that in between intermittent lightning flashes my phallus was visible to her and the sight may have captivated her. Did she feel like Semele, when she saw Zeus in his glory in a flash of light?

The images went away and I was back to reality. She was smiling. Why? She held out her hand and said, "Come with me" . She led me to the porch just outside. It was winter and very cold. She wore a long coat and she quickly buttoned and held it open and whispered, "Times have changed, and so have I" I looked at her slightly protruding belly, and I knew she was with child. She smiled again and said, "It's yours."

My legs felt weak. This was something for which I was not prepared. I was wondering what I should do but I was tongue-tied. It was dark and a drizzle began. I involuntarily took a step forward and all I could do was to caress the slightly protruding belly. How does it feel for a man to be told that this thing has happened? it was after four months and I asked which month is it. I am in the third month she said.

I went on my knees gently lifted the skirt and kissed the slight bulge. She didn't resist and only said this should remain a secret between us. Nobody will know that she and I had made love in the Taj Hotel in Nasik. I said yes but then the next day we went to the lake also.

"Yes," she replied," I remember what a lovely lake. It was so desolate and there was nobody around and it was the monsoon time and that was great fun."

I remember stripping completely nude. She continued standing and then she followed me. She was nude and I could admire her lithe body and flat belly. She followed me into the water and we were soon in waist-deep water It was so chilly and I remember taking her out of the water and carrying her under a tree. What happened under the tree? I think that was the time when Lord Krishna created life in her belly.

I got up and let her skirt fall and then gathered her in my arms. Is there a future I asked. "No," she said, "there is none because right now I'm going to leave the party and go away."

My heart was now beating fast and I had a feeling that it was going to burst out from my breast. Maybe all this was because I was touching 50 and the girl was a good two decades younger.

I wanted to say wait don't go but the words would not come out of my throat. I was mouthing the words but the voice would not come out of my throat. It was as if a paralysis had overtaken my throat and I had lost the power of speech.

She wanted to go away, but then my legs which had been rubbery suddenly became a lot firmer and I launched myself forward and pulled her to me. There was heavy rain all around and thunder was flashing in the sky. "What are you doing?" She whispered.

I didn't say a word as my lips imprisoned her and my tongue forced itself inside her mouth. I was strong, pretty strong. The porch on which we were standing was dark and now lightning was flashing across the sky and a little distance away I could see the lights of the party which was in full swing.

She pushed me away with the words, "I have to go. Your gift must remain secret."

She looked at me with her mouth open and her dark eyes. I laughed and grabbed her head but this time when I touched her something happened in me which made this touch different from any touch earlier in Nasik or the lake.

She did not resist but lay where I had pulled her, against my chest. And I realized that my heart was beating wildly and that Sapna was trembling against me and the darkness lit by flashes of lightning added its aura to the evening.

I started to kiss her and Sapna raised her head as I lowered mine and we kissed. We had our arms around each other. It was like holding some rare, doomed, extinct bird that I had found. I was very frightened; I am not sure but probably she was frightened too, and we shut our eyes. Nothing happened further, and so she untwined herself from me and moved toward the lighted doors, and entered inside the hall. There was a crash of thunder, and I slowly began to move to the lighted doors.

I entered inside and could not see my girl. Probably she had left and then I realized I had seen her for the last time and I was not going to see her again. Now by a quirk of fate here was the same girl sitting. She recognized me and smiled. Is it a sign that the lord had something deeper to convey?

CHAPTER THIRTEEN

FAIZABAD

Memories don't die, but many times in your life, they are rekindled, and one wonders what would have happened if they became real. As part of my ground tenure, I remember being detailed to undergo the provost course. This was part of the service schedule to give a break from flying duties. Air Headquarters nominated me to undergo the. Army Provost Course at the Corps of Military Police, Centre and School at Faizabad. This is a small sleepy town in North India in the state of Uttar Pradesh and is 13 miles from Ayodhya, which is so much in the news these days. The CMP Centre was set up by the British army about 150 years back and a lot of history is attached to this cantonment. Faizabad itself is a small town and it survives because of the cantonment, which is one of the biggest in Uttar Pradesh and has a small river flowing through it, I don't remember the name of the river, but that is not important to the story. I reached Faizabad, a hundred miles from the capital Lucknow, and got down from my compartment and was very happy to note that the Army in the usual spit and polish style had detailed a Hawaladar to receive me. He recognized me instantly, saluted me, and led me to the military jeep to take me to the military school. For the record, there were 20 Officers detailed for this course, and I was the only Air Force officer.

After the formalities, we were all taken to the local cycle shop and each of us was given a bicycle to travel around the cantonment, which was spread over an area of at least 20 miles. I selected a bicycle, after testing, this was to be the mode of conveyance in the military camp for the next six weeks for that is the duration of the course.

I was allotted a nice room in the officer's mess overlooking the river and an orderly to work with me. As I went to sleep, I felt happy that this would be a new experience from the rigors of Air Force duty. The next morning, we were addressed by the commandant and just for the record his name was Colonel Grant, and this was his last posting as he was retiring, and we were told that after retirement was going away to England. He was an Anglo-Indian and probably felt more comfortable going to England, than settling in India.

We soon settled down to our training were addressed by senior police officers and had theory and practical classes. The best part was the regimental cinema hall, which screened pictures from Indian Cinema. The cinema functioned three days a week with one show which commenced at 7 PM. It was an open-air theatre, so the films could only be shown when it was dark. And accordingly, I decided that this was the best way to pass the time in Faizabad.

The first Thursday I cycled to the cinema hall, parked my bicycle outside went inside, and sat in the officer's enclosure, which included seats in the first four rows. I looked around and suddenly my eye saw a lovely young girl entering and sitting just about 4 feet away from me. She was an exhilarating sight, and could not be more than 20. Considering that I was a young man, at the age of 23, my heart jumped to my throat. She was wearing a shalwar and a Kameez (long shirt) and was fair, with her hair pulled back to form a ponytail. This added to her allure. She was a lovely specimen of a girl. Throughout the film, with a cool breeze blowing all around my attention was riveted on the girl and not the film. Honestly, I liked her very much and I could make out that as she sat in the front row, she was an officer's daughter.

My single-minded attention could not have been lost on the girl, and after the interval, she looked at me and smiled. I think that broke the ice and I got up from my seat, sat close to her, and introduced myself. I held out my hand and she shook it and told me that she was a daughter of the Major, who oversaw the security of the cantonment. Her name was Shivendra.

After that, we had a sultry conversation and none of us was interested in the movie, which was by the Indian actor Amitabh Bachchan. I told the girl that I would be coming on Saturday for the movie again, and after that, would she like to come to the Army club?

"Yes," she replied, "We go there quite often, and yes, I will come for the movie on Saturday."

Saturday soon came, and I reached the regimental theatre on my bicycle. I quickly went inside and found that I had come a little early, and nobody was there. I had forgotten in my excitement to meet the girl that I was at least 35 minutes early from the start of the film. I was wondering whether Shivendra would be similarly excited and come early, and I was right. I saw her walking from the entrance and come and sit next to me. There were only two of us in the theatre and I told her straight away, "You're very beautiful."

She looked at me and said, "Thank you, I am a Sikh"

"Fine," I said, "I am also Sikh."

"But you're not a traditional Sikh, as you don't have a turban and beard, and my father wears a turban and beard."

"Yes," I replied, "I was brought up this way, but I'm still a Sikh."

I observed the girl closely and realized she was wonderful with a small bust line, hiding virginal breasts, a slim waist, and a sculpted face. After the film, we kept sitting in the theatre till it emptied, and then she asked me," How are you going to go back?"

"I'm going to go on my bicycle, how are you going back?"

"I generally just walk down because the bungalow is a furlong way."

Without realizing it on the spur, I blurted out, "Why don't you sit on the top tube bar of my cycle, and I'll drop you to your house?"

She was taken aback and was in a bit of a quandary to answer, but I persisted and said," There is nothing to worry about. I'll drop you and go away." "Okay," she said

It was dark now, and she sat on the handlebar of my cycle, and I slowly began to move in the direction of the major's bungalow. It bent forward and the aroma emanating from her body was intoxicating. We soon reached her house, and I dropped her outside and prepared to go away when she said," why don't you come inside and have a soft drink?" I replied, "no, I will be going and left."

Two weeks elapsed and a degree of intimacy developed between me and Shivendra. On Sunday morning, I decided to be brave and cycled down to her house. I knocked and the mother opened the door. She led me to the living room, obviously, her daughter had told her about me, and she motioned me to the sofa and told me that soon Shivendra would join us. The house help brought us two glasses of lime juice and as it was hot, I thought it was good idea to refresh myself with the lime juice. Shivendra came and she looked lovely with shorts, as she had come from the gym. She had beautiful legs, and I realized the beauty of the girl. My eyes riveted on her as she sat down crossing her legs.

"It looks like," I said," you told your mother about me."

"Yes," she replied, "and I also told her that you dropped me on the bicycle the other day." It was a nice meeting, but all good things come to an end, and I left.

We met again at the regimental cinema hall in the evening. After the movie I offered to drop her home and she readily consented. She sat on the handlebar, and I began to pedal forward but this time I pedaled the bike towards the thick cluster of trees, and she looked at me and said where are you taking me?

"No way," I said, "are you frightened?"

"Of course, not," she replied.

We reach the great trees, and I stopped under a large tree and then told her," You are the most beautiful girl I've ever seen, and I don't know whether I can make a proposal for you to your father."

She didn't answer but after a moment said, "my father is a devout Sikh. I don't think he will approve marriage."

Suddenly thunder crashed across the sky and as in north India, heavy rain began to fall, but we were safe under the tree, but were getting wet. The aroma from her body intoxicated me, and for the first time I kissed her eyes. She did not resist, and then I kissed her lips and my tongue, sought the inside of her mouth.

It was a long kiss, and I could make out that this is the first time she had ever been kissed and for me, also, it was the first time. The rain continued to fall, and I hugged her to me. My arms, tightened around her and I imagined that the lord had come to bless us. The trees with the rain thundering all around and the cool breeze blowing I could have had Shivendra for myself. I. never went the whole hog. I do not know why, and I just kissed her and in a swift movement cradled her in my arms, my lips glued to her and sat down on the soft grass. After many minutes, I let go of her and said, "I'm sorry I do not know what will happen in the future, but I must take you back."

I dropped her back at the house, kissed her and went away.

Back in my room, I could not sleep and when I did fall sleep I had a weird dream. I saw Shivendra completely naked riding on a lion. I woke up and realized it was only a dream. I waited for the next screening at the regimental cinema. I reached the cinema hall, but this time my girl was not there. I moved around and then left the movie midway and took the cycle and went across to her house. I found the lights were off, and I asked the watchman where had the Major are gone. He said he has been transferred and has left.

"And his family?"

"They left along with him"

I turned the bicycle back and headed back to the mess. I had no desire to watch the film in the theatre. The only question I was thinking was why she not told me that her father was already under orders and was going away. If she had told me maybe the story would have been different. One cannot say what may have happened because there is also a good chance that the Major would not have accepted me, as I was not a Sikh with the traditional look. Maybe that was the reason.

Faizabad remains a memory in my mind a fleeting memory. The fact is, I finished my course and went back to the Air Force and the Major, and his daughter became Just a memory something to remember.

CHAPTER FOURTEEN

OLD DREAMS AND DREALITY

A few days back, I had been to a café by the roadside in Mumbai with a friend. The monsoon season was beginning, and there were dark clouds all around. It was getting dark, and I had a feeling It would rain. The café had a small tent extending from the front and housed, a few tables. It is great fun to sit in such an atmosphere slightly protected from the rain and at the same time, savour the delight of the Mumbai monsoon. I sat down and looked at the menu and found that most dishes were from the Orient. That's fine because I do have a penchant for Oriental food. The rain was now picking up momentum and I along with my friend was sitting and enjoying the monsoon showers as they beat on the earth. A waiter appeared. I looked at him and was surprised to note that he was from the North East. I looked at him and asked him," What is your name?"

He replied," Sir, Harry." That meant he was a Christian and now I knew he had to be from one of the states of the Northeast. "Which state do you belong to?" I asked. He replied," Nagaland."

Nagaland is one of the most beautiful states of the Indian Union. It's a small hilly state with thick forests and people of short stature, but generally fair and more kinship with the Burmese and Thais.

I was delighted that the waiter was from Nagaland, and I closed my eyes as I was reminded of an incident that had occurred years back. Memories die hard, but this meeting with the waiter from Nagaland ignited a lamp from the past.

I remember, driving down the road from Jorhat to Dimapur in Nagaland. Dimapur is a cosmopolitan city connected by rail to all parts of India. The drive to Dimapur was splendour personified in a one-ton Jonga. Our driver now pulled up outside a small eating joint. I will call it an 'eating joint' because it serves a mixture of food and drink. The driver halted and said," Sir, this is a place to have a break before we enter Dimapur; after that, we can continue to, Mokekchung."

I and my two companions both NCOs entered the small café constructed of bamboo sticks. We sat at an empty table and waited for someone to attend to us. I was aware of the peculiarity of the hill states where almost all the eating joints and bars are managed by women, and the men are rarely seen. One wonders where the men are as women do everything.

We had not long to wait when a middle-aged lady came and said," You all seem to be from the military. I know it, and for you, I have got some good Army Rum."

I smiled at her and said, "That is wonderful, which Rum is it"

She replies, "It's Hercules."

Krishna's arrow

Hercules is a popular brand in the services, and after I nodded my approval, a beautiful young girl, brought two glasses with the red colour elixir. I looked at the girl and immediately liked her. She wore a short skirt and a loose blouse that showcased a pair of sculpted legs.

After we had finished drinking and eating roast chicken, we got up to leave when the lady came up to me and said," You seem to be the man in charge, my daughter has to get to our village close to Mokekchung and would like that you give her a lift in your vehicle.

I think the lady was sure that I would agree because the girl was ready with a small bag; ready to go. I smiled at the lady and said," It's okay, she can travel in the Jonga with me." She got into the front seat with me.

We drove towards Dimapur and were into an animated conversation. She told me she had been to college in Imphal and had just landed a job. She also told me that she had got a job in Shillong in the Air Force canteen as a salesgirl. She was happy as she would get   ₹5000 a month. In those days it was a princely sum. I looked at the girl and said, "We will stop at Dimapur for the night, and then go onto Mokekchung."

"Yes," she said, "I anticipated it but I don't like Dimapur."

The ice was broken between us, and what stood out was a captivating smile. She was very fair, and I guessed her age could not be more than 22 or 23.

The Jonga made good progress and we were soon entering the city. The driver stopped the car at the GREF camp and I told my NCOs to get down and spend the night there as I would be going, to the officer's mess of the Assam Rifles.

I told the driver to take us to the camp of the Assam rifles. After the verification at the guard room, we went to the officer's mess. The Mess Havildar met us and said, "We did not know that you were coming with your wife, Sir I have allotted a single room and there is no other room available."

The Havildar continued, "We are sorry that we have only one room available now as many visiting officers visiting as General Officer Commanding is visiting this area. I hope you can stay in the single room."

I looked at the girl and said, "Is it okay?"

She smiled, and replied, "Yes, it's fine."

Outside, as we all know in the northeast, the wettest place on earth, the monsoon had picked up and now beat on the earth. I opened the window and looked out and saw a lake and the surrounding jungle. I couldn't see much further because the visibility was poor with the heavy rain.

"It's a beautiful place," I said

"Yes," she replied, "but I am waiting to get to Shillong."

It was evening, and I rang up the Mess caterer and told him, we would like to eat food in our room and could arrange to send the items here. He said yes, sir, not a problem because the dining hall is booked for the general Sahib".

I looked at the girl and said, "Okay, you can change into something comfortable."

She opened her suitcase selected a dress, went into the washroom, and returned. She looked more beautiful as she wore shorts and a loose T-shirt. I wondered whether she knew of the effect she was having on me.

The room opened onto a small porch, which was half covered. She opened the door and I saw that it was raining heavily, and she screamed," I always Love the rain."

With these words, she just went out into the rain. I watched, and after some time she returned. I told her why she went into the rain and was wet. The blouse was sticking to her body, and I could make out that she had to remove her bra. The small bust was straining at the T-shirt.

I said," You better take off that T-shirt."

"I don't have another one."

"I will give you one, but probably it will be oversized."

I gave one to her, and then surprisingly, there was no sense of shame as he just turned her back to me, removed her shirt, and from the back, I could make out a slim waist, she put on the shirt and then turned to face me.

"You're beautiful," I said

"I know," she replied, "but unfortunately, I don't like the Naga men they always get drunk. Don't do any work."

We drank the rum and ate the food, and after that, I think Lord Krishna took a hand. Thunder was crashing all around with lightning flashing across the sky. I took a step forward, pulled her wet shorts down and, and was witness to the most feminine part of her body. What forward next was a hedonistic delight. Needless to say, it was a night without end, the atmosphere, the rain, and the wheel of gold. All played their part and by morning we had eaten the forbidden apple. It was still raining early morning when I got up and rang up for the bed tea. I gently woke the girl and brought her a cup of tea and we drank it.

We spent another two hours before we got into the Jonga and then headed for our destination. During the second part of the drive, we never spoke much except that I kept holding her and all the time. I remember the rain continued, and the driver told us, "Sir, this is the monsoon. I suggest there is Paul's café coming. We better stop there."

He pulled the Car in front of a wooden shack and both of us entered. The driver kept sitting in the Jonga and an old lady realized we wanted 2 cups of tea. "How far are we from Mokekchung," I asked. The lady replied that it was about 10 miles, maybe another half-hour drive, but you better wait till the monsoon finishes.

There were no words spoken as I just took the girl's hand and went into the small portico at the back of the back, shut the door, and now nobody could see us except the jungle. I pulled her shorts down and the inevitable happened.

Later we got in the car and soon reached our destination. She gave us directions to a small house and got down there and said," Thank you for the lift. I don't think I will ever miss you."

old-dreams-and-reality

She went inside and I drove away to the Army camp. Well time does pass and I reached Shillong a few months later, and I thought I should check up whether this girl was still working in the Air Force canteen. I reached the Canteen and asked about any Naga girls, the manager told me yes, but she worked only for three months and after that, the USA AID gave her a job and she left for America

I just smiled and left. I closed my eyes sitting in the café as the waiter brought the items which we had ordered. My friend looked at me and said, "Look, pal. I think you went into a reverie."

"Yes, I said, seeing the waiter reminded me of something."

"I hope it was something good"

"It was something wonderful,"

At the back of my mind. I was just wondering what happened. Could it have been a reality? A dream? I also remember never using any protection and wondered whether my seed could have fertilized her. These are the questions that came into my mind, as the monsoon gathered strength. I ate the food with my friend and the evening passed.

CHAPTER FIFTEEN

USHA

There comes a time in a man's life when he faces what is called the moment of truth, I think this is something that every man and woman faces. This is a tale of a man who was faced with this moment of truth in his life and failed at that moment.

Jimmy had landed at Goa. He was on his way to the Taj Exotica a wonderful hotel owned by the Taj group close to Varca Beach. Here was a married man with one child who he had left behind so that the son's schooling would not be disturbed. He has travelled alone to take up his appointment as the Director. As he came out of the airport, he found a man standing with a placard with his name. It was obvious the hotel administration had sent the man to receive him. He walked up to the man and said," I am Jimmy."

"Yes sir, I have to take you to the hotel, and as desired by you a room has been reserved."

He saw Jimmy's bag in the trolley, lifted it, and said. "Sir, please come with me ." He led him to the Toyota and opened the back door for Jimmy to slide in. Goa is the pleasure house of the western coast. It is no surprise that most of the clientele the visitors and tourists are from Eastern Europe. Why Eastern Europe? because that is the less affluent part of Europe and people who want to enjoy a budget holiday with the beach, and the sun will choose Goa.

The drive was Inevitable, and Jimmy was able to observe the beautiful landscape and the sea. He could see the pristine waters as they crashed against the rocks. The car pulled up to the foyer of the hotel, and there was a party waiting outside consisting of the executive manager, and some other staff who had been informed that the new director was coming.

The pleasantries were exchanged, and Jimmy told the manager," Let's get down to brass tacks, as you are aware I am an ex-military officer, and I am very keen to get a grip on this work, so would you kindly ask all the managers to report to me right away so we can have the introduction and I can get a grip of the hotel administration"

The meeting went very well, and he had a look at the financial statistics and realized that the hotel was not doing very well. Out of the seven managers, he saw that one of them was a woman. He had enough knowledge of the demographics of the country having travelled all over the country to understand that the girl or maybe it's better to use the word woman because she could be about 30+ was a Brahmin from the state of Tamil Nadu.

She had already introduced herself as Usha and informed she was the chief executive housekeeper. Now this is a very important job, and it's incumbent on the executive housekeeper to organize the maintenance of all the rooms and the linen to impeccable standards.

Jimmy wondered why he uttered the words but he did utter," Usha you better step back for a minute I have some important information to ask you."

He realized he had nothing important to ask except that he liked Usha very much. She was slim and wore a sari tied low down the navel and overall looked extremely exotic like most Brahmin girls from Tamil Nādu. She had smouldering, doe-brown eyes, and a queenly figure.

She was relatively fit and nubile and she reminded him of a gazelle.

She had already got up to leave but now walked back to the chair opposite his table. Jimmy liked the way she walked. He also noticed her smooth complexion. Maybe she was using a lot of fair and lovely cream. She had almost virginal breasts and he liked her immensely. She sat down and asked," Yes sir what is it you want to know."

Jimmy just sat and looked at her wondering what to say. All he said was, " I asked you to stay back because I have something important to discuss with you."

'Yes sir"

"I want to know the status of the rooms in the hotel, and how you go about getting the housekeeping done. Give me all the details."

Usha replied, "I gave you most of the details, but I will repeat the," and she repeated everything. She mentioned she had 40 girls on the housekeeping staff with two supervisors and she was the chief executive. She also mentioned that she had been working in the hotel for three years.

Jimmy then said," I'm going to have a cup of tea. I want you to join me." Usha could make out that Jimmy was fair and muscular. Add his age of 40 years didn't show on him.

Usha laughed and said," Sir, you are the Director and it's my pleasure to have a cup of tea with you. I will just pass the message on the mobile to the caterer on duty to bring good Darjeeling tea. I have a hunch you like Darjeeling tea, which is a little mild, but it has its own flavour."

"Wonderful it's something that I love".

The meeting over the cup of tea continued for two hours, and Usha began to realize what a wonderful man the Director was. The very fact that he was a Punjabi, fair and tall and macho has its own effect. No wonder that most of the heroes of Bombay films are from Punjab.

The conversation soon meandered away from official work to personal work and Usha told her everything that she was married but divorced. She also told him that it was an unhappy marriage, but that is all that she said, After that, they talked of everything under the sun and stars.

The days now began to pass and Jimmy got into the groove. The hotel also began to feel the change of command, and the staff became more motivated. Jimmy had offered to stay in the hotel, and he didn't want to take a flat outside. In that case, he would be 24 hours on duty and would be able to monitor the functioning of the hotel.

The Hindu festival of Diwali came and Jimmy sat In his room, wondering what to do he had just spoken to his son, and he was relieved that the boy was happy. on an impulse, he decided to call Usha.

She came and as she entered the apartment, the perfume that she was using permeated to Jimmy. She also looked exotic in a gold embroidered Sari and a low-cut blouse. In short, she looked extremely sexy and attractive and then he saw a burn mark on the neck. He wondered why he hadn't noticed it earlier.

During the last three months, Jimmy and Usha have been working together, rather he was the boss and she the assistant. He had plenty of time to study her anatomy and realize she had an Amazonian figure that sat well on her slim body. During this period the two were thrown together and soon Usha realized that Jimmy was interested in her. She also likes Jimmy. The two vibe and this soon becomes intense, but perhaps both of them are scared of the consequences. Today is Diwali and she had entered his office. Jimmy looked at her and said," I hope you won't mind a question?"

" What is it?"

"Can you tell me how you got that burn mark on your neck?"

There was a moment of silence and outside the lights were twinkling. It was late at night, the entire hotel had been on their toes for the Diwali function. She was silent for a moment and then said in a flat voice," My husband did it. He would apply the cigarette butts all over my body, and then I could take it no longer, left him and now I'm here."

The words had an aphrodisiac effect on Jimmy. He got up from his chair and walked up to her and kissed her eyes and then the burn mark on her neck and said," I wonder how anybody can be so foolish, but I am not going to the details as today is Diwali, the festival of lights."

She looked at him quizzically, "You are a different sort of a man I wonder what you are thinking."

"You are sure, you want to know?"

She was silent for a moment perhaps debating what to say. Jimmy did not wait for an answer and said, "I want to see you as God has created you."

There was a deafening silence and from kissing her eyelids he moved to her lips.

His heart is pulsating pumping blood to his brain. As the lips of Usha open he realizes he is the lion and he is going to tame the lioness.

He just lifted her from her seat and carried her to the couch at one end. He sensed his advantage and without a protest removed her sari, blouse, and petticoat. He was in for a shock to observe burn marks on her buttocks, and he kissed each of them softly.

She had a decanter-shaped waist and her complexion was smooth and impeccable. Her pencil-thin eyebrows eased down gently to her black, long eyelashes. She could have been the joy of a sculptor. Her smile, was beguiling, showing peal white teeth. It lit up the room like an electric current. Filed to perfection, her fingernails ran through her black hair. She had a photogenic face and hid a swan's neck, elegant and smooth. Jimmy loved her black eyes which sparkled.

Her lips tasted like rose petals. It surprised him that they were plump and sweet. She had a demure, timorous personality. She whispered to him in a voice as sweet as any songbird. Her body odour lingered in the room and he felt intoxicated.

Did Jimmy kiss her? Yes, he did and it was a hedonistic delight. He unfastens the hooks of her blouse and slowly rolls the sari of her hips. Her petticoat is next and then her underwear. She opens her eyes as her hand touches his chest. She takes him in her hand and the ritual starts, she accepts without a word.

It is half an hour before they fall apart, it was something inevitable, and soon his seed had flown into her body.

Many days passed, and now it was a regular occurrence. His need for her was intense and she was like a hungry lioness always wanting more. One day they lay in bed coupled together, She looked at him and said softly," Would you marry me?"

The realization dawned on Jimmy that an impossible situation had been created.

The words were like a stone bringing him back to his senses. The enormity of the situation overwhelmed him. He kissed her eyes and asked, "Why what has happened?"

He dreaded the answer as Usha whispered," I am carrying your baby"

He didn't know what to answer and all he could blurt out was, "I think you already know that I'm married."

She didn't say a word just got up, wore her clothes, and said, "I'm glad in a way that you are truthful. I will just fade away from your life."

She left him and the door shut after she left. Jimmy, wanted to stop her, but his legs would not move, and the words would not come out of his mouth. He drank the whole night. His mind was clearer the next day and he resolved to find a solution. The next morning he reached the office and asked his secretary, "Can you ask Usha to come ." His mind was now clear that he would not forsake her and he longed to meet her again. Yes, he would gather her in his arms, kiss her and tell her that he would be by her side.

The secretary looked at him and said, "Sir, she has packed her bags and left and has handed her resignation letter to me."

There was nothing Jimmy could do. He felt a sense of immense loss. Jimmy never met Usha again. Many years later he came to know that maybe she had gone to Canada but that was all.

CHAPTER SIXTEEN

THE ETIGER

It was 1913, the Raj was omnipotent over India and in Madhya Pradesh, a forest officer moved among the villages and the thick jungles. He was an English man who had spent all his life in India, and never seen the face of England. In his way, he liked India and the people and the jungles and joined the Indian Forest Service. He was the Burra Sahib, the big white hunter who saved the villagers from the ferocious maneaters who were sometimes moving around. His name was Harry Savage and he had a girlfriend who was an Anglo-Indian named Barbara who resided in Nagpur. He was close friends with another Anglo-Indian named John. Unknown to Harry, John loved Barbara, and many times he was consumed with anger and hate against Harry because Barbara preferred Harry over him.

Harry was sitting in the veranda of his bungalow and far away he observed a jeep approaching and he guessed it must be. John. His orderly Ram Singh sat on the floor beside him. The jeep pulled up and John jumped out and said, "Harry. I've got some news for you."

"What's up, pal?"

"War clouds are over Europe and the government wants the maximum number of able-bodied men to join the Army to fight the Germans."

"Good what's your planning"

"I think we should both enlist and after the war is over, we can come back."

" Splendid idea," Harry replied, " both of us will go, but before that, I must go and meet Barbara."

"Oh yes, I had forgotten," at the same time he was consumed with anger, but it didn't show on his face.

John left immediately, and Harry got into his jeep and drove to Nagpur. He took Ram Singh along with him. He reached in the evening and straightaway drove to the residence of Barbara. He knocked on the door and opened it. Barbara was standing before him. She rushed to his arms, and both kissed spontaneously. in between the kisses, she whispered," It's so nice that you have come."

"Anybody at home,?", he asked.

"No one at the moment as Dad has gone to the workshop and Mom to the Local Club." Harry lifted Barbara in his arms and with soft kisses carried her into the bedroom." What are you doing?" she whispered.

He smiled and said," I want to love you because tomorrow I am going to enlist in the army and go to Europe to fight the Germans and John also is coming with me." Harry laid her on the bed. His mind is melting fast, his soul is whispering I love you, his eyes are begging please and she sees lust in them. He whispers, "Let me undress you, caress your skin, and massage your back".

He had taken off her dress and now it lay crumpled on the floor. Barbara was a thrilling sight as he saw her in her most intimate clothing. This was only the beginning, and he put his hands in the elastic of her panty and pulled it down, even as his hands moved up to unhook the bra, his lips glued to Barbara's. Much later, as he moved furiously he realized she was a virgin and it was not long before he deposited his seed. As he crumpled over her, at the back of his mind was the thought, what if Barbara conceived?

harry-and-his-love-and-
the-tiger

POW camp

Both Harry and John joined the regiment, and soon they were in the thick of battle. In one battle, the Germans struck under cover of heavy artillery, and though the British were fighting back, they were outnumbered. To cut a long story short both Harry and John were taken POW. They were housed in a large camp and the Security was a little lax. The leader Colonel Hopkins made the escape plan and said," Six of us will break out from the camp and perhaps the Germans will not detect for some time because there are almost 1000 of us here. Bear in mind that one of us will flash a torch after all six are out of the camp, this will signal the resistance fighters, who will take us to safety."

John volunteers to be the man who will flash the torch. But when all the men had gone past the perimeter and only Harry had been left, John flashed the torch. The searchlight picked up Harry and the machine gun opened fire. The bullet hit Harry in his left leg and he couldn't move forward John and the others escaped leaving Harry behind. John had seen the machine gun firing, and he was pretty sure that Harry would be dead.

The Germans picked up Harry and took him to the hospital where the doctor gave the bad news that his leg below the knee would have to be amputated. Harry remained a prisoner of war, but he recovered and was given a false foot and he was almost 90% normal. At the end of the war, he came back and landed in Bombay. He had sent a letter to Ram Singh asking If he could come and meet him at Apollo Bundar. When he came out he saw Ram Singh standing. He was crying when he saw Harry and said "Sahib what happened we thought you were dead." Harry embraced Ram Singh and said, "It doesn't matter Ram. I am glad that you have come but now I will go back to the forest office in Madhya Pradesh. The job has been given back to me. Will you again work with me? There were tears in the eyes of Ram Singh and he said, "Sir, that will be the greatest honour for me."

As they sat in the Victoria which was to take them to the Bombay Victoria rail terminus, he asked Ram Singh, "You haven't told me anything about Barbara." Ram Singh with tears said, "Sahib we were told you had died and probably Barbara Madam also was given this information and she married John Sahib" He didn't say anything and soon they had boarded the Calcutta Mail. The news of Harry joining back as the DFO spread like wildfire and there was relief among the villagers that the great white Shikari had come back because they were now being terrorized by a tiger who had already eaten 12 villagers.

Barbara also heard the news and she confronted John. "You had told me that Harry is no more and you had seen him die. I want to meet this man. Is he alive?"

"I don't know"

"I want to meet him"

John thought for a moment and said, "Okay I will take you to him, but I am pretty sure this man is an impostor."

They reached the bungalow, and John was praying that it would not be Savage, but someone else, but the moment he saw him his heart sank as he recognized the man, but he was now limping because his foot had been amputated. Barbara also saw Harry her heart beating widely. She thought of her four-year-old boy who was the son and she was confused.

Harry welcomed both of them into the living room and said, "You both wait here because I am on my way to kill a tiger- a maneater."

"Are you going alone?" Barbara asked

"No Ram Singh will accompany me. He is the only faithful man I have in the world."

John looked at Harry and said, "May I also come with you for the hunt?"

"Yes you can, but please obey every order that I tell you don't like the last time flash the torch before it was required"

Barbara heard this conversation and the realization dawned on her that John had engineered the capture of Harry and she hated him. She was glad that she had not allowed John to touch her, and the marriage had been one of convenience to give a name to the boy, She wondered if she could convince Harry.

Finale

Ram Singh, returned with the jeep and Harry got in the front seat with his elephant rifle. John sat at the back and they drove out into the jungle. After driving a few miles, they stopped and Ramu said," Sahib, we will now go on foot. I can see the pugmarks of the tiger and will lead you to the beast."

"You wait here John till we come back"

"No," John replied," I'll come with you"

All the three now entered the jungle and Ram Singh expertly tracked the Tiger. They reached a point and stopped. Ram said," Sir, The pug marks have ended here, that means the tiger is around here, you take over Sahib."

Harry looked around and saw 2 rocks, and he said," We will hide behind those rocks and wait for the tiger to come because he will come as he needs human flesh".

They positioned themselves behind the rocks, and Harry said," Nobody will fire till the Tiger comes within range."

After waiting for half an hour, they saw the magnificent beast emerge from the jungle. His skin was shining but he was limping and Harry guessed the reason the beast had become a man-eater but now he had no choice. He would have to kill the animal and he waited for the beast to come.

John's mind was working feverishly, and he decided to have a last chance. He fired a bullet from his rifle.

Harry shouted at John. "What have you done you have alerted the tiger. "The tiger now came running towards Harry. It was a split-second movement and he fired at the tiger. Two shots hit him in between the eyes. He was always a master shot. The tiger had reached Harry and swiped at him. The claw cut his chest, but he did not die.

Ram Singh ran to Harry saw the blood on his shirt and said, "Sir are you okay? the Tiger has clawed you."

"It's nothing, I will recover."

John also came and said," I'm sorry I just panicked."

John kept looking at Harry, his eyes betrayed him, and he knew the truth. He didn't say anything, and both the men helped him into the jeep, and they drove to the local hospital. The British surgeon attended immediately, and after he had examined him, just smiled, "These are superficial wounds, you will recover, but it would have been touch and go if you hadn't hit the tiger between the eyes but man tell me who is the man who elected to fire at the tiger."

Harry didn't say anything but only looked at John. That look conveyed a lot to the surgeon. John quickly left the scene with the words, "Harry. I will come later". As John left, Barbara entered the chamber, and she was crying," I'm so glad that you killed the tiger. I knew you could do it because you are something special.'

"Thank you"

"Harry, I want to tell you something which has been in my mind. After that, you can decide what you want to do. When you had gone away, I was told you had died and I was in the family way, there was nothing to do because otherwise, it would be a great stigma, so once John told me he had seen you die, I married him with the condition that he would not touch me till I was sure you are dead."

"What made you think that I had not died"

"It's a silly thing but in the jungle, there is a small hamlet where an ancient baba sits, a Hindu priest who is supposed to divine and look into the future. I went to this man and he looked at me and said without my asking a question,' *My daughter, the man you love will come, he is not dead wait for him,* If you don't believe me, Harry, I will go away. Otherwise, please come to Nagpur with me and meet your son."

Harry got up from his chair and Barbara saw that he strapped his support. She saw the amputated foot as he strapped, the artificial foot and briskly began to walk out. The surgeon says, "You need some more rest."

"No, doctor," he replied," I don't need any, I want to meet my son.'

What about John nobody heard of him and many wondered if he had gone to Australia or maybe even the Pacific islands because now he could never show his face to the Anglo-Indian community. He vanished.

After the reunion, Harry carried Barbara, like last time to the bed, opened up her blouse and his face between the hallway of the breasts, and said "It's about time my son had a brother."

CHAPTER SEVENTEEN

THE HOSTAGE

The city was in ferment, crowds of young men were roaming the streets, shouting slogans like *death to Satan* and *victory for us.* The ruler had fled the country and there was all-around anarchy. In the embassy, 10 marines, waited, apprehensively as crowds, numbering, thousands chanting, deadly slogans swarmed around the compound. How many were there? John one of the marines, has his finger on the automatic's trigger as he wonders what he should do. He was pretty sure that in case the crowd broke into the compound, he would be dead. That would be the last time he would breathe. He was praying to God that the crowd would go away but it was not likely that they would go away and he was pretty sure they would soon come and they came. They entered the compound broke the iron Gate, and soon a couple of men had come and taken them away. He was wondering what his government would do. He didn't fire his rifle which is a wise thing to do and soon he was loaded into a half truck and taken away.

They drove along the dusty roads and stopped before a large house, and one of the guards could be heard shouting. "Keep this man here, the others we will keep in different places." Another man shouted," Why not imprison them all together?" "Don't argue," the man replies," these are the instructions, this marine has to be kept hostage."

John was a bodybuilder with biceps that bulged to 16 inches and a perfect specimen of a human being. Man to man he could have thrown any of the attackers away, but since there were tens of them, he knew it would be a foolish thing to do.

He was taken inside the building and put inside a room and then he heard the lock outside, he knew that he had been taken hostage. He wondered what had happened to his friends, but now he couldn't think of what to do.

He had a look around the room. It was bare except for one blanket on the floor. There was a toilet attached to it and that was the saving grace. Otherwise, there was a small window with an iron drill and a door that had been locked. He sat on the floor and thought what would happen. Outside, he could hear some voices, and now he realized they were women. The door opened and a woman in a hijab stood before him. She held a rifle, looked at him, and said, "My friend was right. You are a bodybuilder."

John didn't answer. He kept quiet and remained sitting on the floor. The woman who entered inside lifted the veil from her face and John saw something that thrilled him. He saw a beautiful face with large eyes and a milk complexion. Her body was covered with the black cloak and he couldn't make out anything else.

"Get up," the woman ordered, "and stand"

John didn't want to create any trouble and stood up.

As John got up the woman sucked in her breath as John reminded her of a massive tiger with his pectorals showing through his shirt and half-cut sleeves bringing out the bulge of biceps. He was almost like the God Apollo in all his glory.

The woman shut the door from inside and told John," Now that I am alone, will you attack me?"

John smiled, "I think you have not understood me. I would never lay hands on a woman and in any case you are so beautiful."

Colour came on the cheeks of the woman and she said, "Don't talk nonsense. I only came to see you because one of my friends told me that you were a perfect specimen of a human being, a bodybuilder. My friend told me that you are perhaps like the great Rustam.

"Why have you kept me in this room?:

"It is not my wish, but that of the leader, the supreme leader, and I do not know how long they will keep you here but your other friends are being kept at a different place but I'm afraid you are going to be kept here to pay for the crimes of the man who ruled us. You are lucky that women are going to guard you because the men are busy getting ready for war."

John smiled and said, "Wonderful, You want to hold me accountable for something I have nothing to do with."

"I will advise you not to talk nonsense. Let me know if you need anything though my commander wants to put a bullet in your brain."

"Why don't you do it?"

"I will not do it because I don't believe in this revolution. They treat women like cattle now you wait here I will get you some food to eat."

Gods will

After a few hours, he could hear the lock turning outside and the same woman entered. She brought a tray placed it on the floor and told John," Eat this."

John looked at the tray and found it well stocked.

"You have brought good food," he said.

The woman was now pensive and said, " I was told to give you some dry rice and curry but I have brought other things for you because I am a person who believes in God and I don't want to do anything that goes against the will of the Almighty, I cannot treat you like they want me to treat you."

After John had eaten, he got up and said, "Thank you." She pulled out a flask from her hijab and gave it to him. You can drink this. It is juice."

"Why are you doing all this?"

The woman replied, "Don't ask stupid questions."

15 days passed and most of the time the same woman would come to feed him. One day from the small window, he could make out that there was a thunderstorm. It was raining heavily. He looked at the woman and said, "You've come so many times, but you haven't told me your name.:

She paused for a moment and said, "Laila."

After a moment she said, "You have a wonderful body."

John was intrigued and asked," How do you know you haven't seen me."

"Yes, I have," she said, "I have several times watched from the window outside and seen you the way God has made you. I have not seen anybody so well-endowed and muscular as you."

He had begun to like the girl, and now he took a step forward, and in one moment swept her off her feet and kissed her. His mind was in a whirl. What the hell was he doing; kissing a girl who was his guard?

"Don't", she said, but there was no conviction in her voice, and at that time she could think of only what she had seen from the window. He reminded her of the mightiest warrior of Iran, who had been rumoured to have deflowered 80 virgins in one night.

He put Laila on the floor beside him and asked, "Are you not scared that somebody will see you? They would not like you to cohabit with a man who has been taken as a hostage."

"There will be hell to play I cannot help myself. However I have decided to put my desires away and put a bullet in your brain but before that, you can have one last wish."

John thought momentarily and replied, "You claim you have seen me from the window. My wish is that I see you similarly."

Outside thunder and lightning were flashing from the sky and Laila got up. She was shaking," I can't do it." She murmured.

"But you asked me my last wish and if you're going to kill me, you might as well do it."

She moved fast and unloosened the elastic and the gown fell to the floor. She was naked before him and her beauty struck John. He took in her breasts, so shaped like pears, crowned by a luxurious growth on the mons.

Laila was wondering what had come over and she said," I am going to wear my clothes back, and the only way I can kill desire is to put a bullet in your brain."

He was like a tiger and pushed her to the floor, buried his face at the altar of her beauty, and paid his homage to the most esoteric part of Laila's body

Something strange happened and she arched her back to accommodate John. She was wondering what had come over her to have given herself to the hostage. She held the phallus in her hand and its intrinsic strength thrilled her

One thing led to another and she felt she had been taken to the top of Mount Everest. She could see the entire earth below. Something so fulfilling that she would die to eat this fruit again and again. She had some difficulty initially, but soon accommodated him, and both of them were now in the land of bliss. It was much later that she realized that she had given herself to the hostage. She was in a panic now, and as to what she had done and wondered if the revolutionary guards came to know about it, they would kill him and her.

She was too far down the path of pleasure, and she marvelled at the fact that even after the bout, there would be an encore.

She went away after kissing him softly, saying I will come again, but do not tell this to anybody.

Escape

Two months elapsed and it was a daily occurrence. As far as Laila was concerned she would come daily, remove the hijab, and apply her lips to John. The realization dawned on John that he had fallen in love with his guard, but what could he do? One day John noticed that Laila was very quiet, quieter than usual. He realized that she was a little tense. "What has happened,?" he asked

She thought for a moment and said almost in a whisper," I think I've signed my death warrant"

"How is that?"

Laila replied, "I am with child. It is a criminal act for which there is no mercy, I will be stoned to death."

John gathered her in his arms and said, "Do not worry. There is always a way out. If we can escape from here with your help we can reach the border."

"I do not know," she said, "I am very scared."

"Don't worry he said, " I am going to save you." His heart went out to her and desire also overcame him and he had now decided that he would escape with this girl to freedom. He began to kiss her, and what followed, was hedonistic love. This was his most satisfying time as he realized his complete power over Laila. She responded to him like a violin and afterward, both had sex and then lay in each other's arms while outside the thunderstorm raged. He kissed her eyelids and whispered, "We will take our chance and escape right now. I will take you away from here. Let's plan, how many guards are there?"

"There are two revolutionary guards at the gate."

"Don't worry, I will take care of them, but you have to come now with me." She dressed up, opened the door, and came out. She shouted.

"I am coming out"

The guards replied," Okay, lock the door and leave the hostage inside."

John and the girl moved out slowly, and before the guards could do anything two mighty blows from the bodybuilder, and both the garden slumped onto the floor. They moved quickly to the jeep parked outside

Laila whispered, "Take off, the jacket of one of the men and wear it. You will look like a revolutionary guard." Jim brought all his experience to work, removed the shirt of the man with its insignia and left his shirt behind, sat in the jeep, and began to drive them out of the city

The jeep had a clear run as nobody could anticipate that it was John who was driving. There was nobody to stop them and very soon they had left the city and were on the road, they were heading now toward the sea. Jim knew the roads and they made good progress.

They reached the shore of the Sea. How would they go from here? Laila was exhausted and he carried her to a tree, led her onto the soft sand and they kissed like guilty lovers. They kiss innumerable times and then John sees a small fishing boat. Nobody is there and with all his strength pushes the boat into the sea puts Laila into the boat and jumps in. They are on their way to freedom. The escape from the city to the sea was itself a great adventure which I will relate to next. But they were picked by a warship and taken to safety. What happened next is another story.

CHAPTER EIGHTEEN

RIVER OF NO RETURN

1857 was a terrible time in the subcontinent. The East India Company Army had mutinied. British officers had been shot dead and some atrocities had been committed by the sepoys on the families of the Britishers. The worst affected were the cantonments of Lucknow and Kanpur followed by Meerut. These were the main garrisons of the East India Company Army. Bhim Singh was a soldier of the 9th Regiment of the Bengal Army. He had earlier taken part in battle along with the East India Company Army in the North-West frontier at Alkazi but now was stationed in a small Garrison close to the river Ganga. He had got up In the morning and could see the river Ganga as it flowed serenely to the Bay of Bengal. But his mind was in turmoil and he had seen smoke rising some distance away. This was a sign the soldiers of the East India Army had run amuck. There were all sorts of rumours floating around as to why the mutiny had taken place and many had opined that the Britishers were out to destroy the belief of the sepoys in Hinduism and Islam. Bhim did not believe this, he had served under many British officers and he remembered that Lieutenant of the British Army John Saxon had risked his life to rescue him from a horde of Muslims who were out to cut his throat. After he had been saved, and the battle was over, he thanked Lieutenant John Saxon, but the captain had only replied, "It is my job my man to save you."

These words were ringing in the ears of Bhima. He got up, and came out of his billet and found the Subedar Major standing. He came up to Bhima and said, "We must get ready and attack the residency at Lucknow."

"What purpose will it serve?"

"Idiot. These people have defiled our religion by giving us cartridges lined with the lard of cows and pigs, and they must all be killed."

"How are you sure about this bit of wisdom that cartridges are greased with lard of cows and pigs."

Subedar Major got angry. He said ,"you don't know a damn thing. I know everything now we have to immediately attack the residency before the white troops come there. So don't argue, get ready and fall in with your rifle along with the other soldiers and we will forward."

Bhim felt uneasy, and wanted to say no. He had no wish to attack the residency which housed the families of the British officers.

The residency was about 10 miles away. Bhim reluctantly along with his rifle stood along with his platoon. The Subedar Major was looking at them. He was Sher Khan and after a moment paused and said, " the job is done, the sixth platoon attacked the residency and four British women are killed. This is the news so at the moment we will stay put here till we get orders where to go."

Bhima looked at Sher Khan incredibly and asked, "what is the use of killing the woman ,has any one escaped.?"

"Yes," Sher Khan replied," I think one girl has escaped and is on the run in the countryside."

" Why our soldiers killed the women, that is not what Dharma says."

"Don't teach me, Dharma, otherwise, I'll court martial and hang you on the nearest tree."

Bhim was quiet. The platoon disbanded, everybody went their way, and Bhim decided that he would walk towards the Residency. His mind was in some turmoil as he thought about the young girl who had escaped from there, and what would happen to her if she fell fall into the hands of the sepoys.

The sun was rising, and a golden glow was all around. The Ganga was looking calm and placid. He divested himself of his clothes and jumped into the river and swam around lazily. After that, he came out, dressed and began to walk towards the Residency from which he could still see the smoke rising

All around, there were a lot of trees, and small woods, and knew that some of them housed the panther and other wildlife. His thoughts reverted to the time he had been saved by his company commander in the battle at Orkazi .Such men could not defile his religion. It was a lot of bullshit and didn't believe it.

He stood under a tree with his rifle, and then he was all alert for he heard the unmissable sound of a cough. Instinct told him it was a girl and he began to look around. He was sure that they was someone in the thicket, and he resolved to solve the mystery. He pushed aside some bushes and low and behold he saw a young girl, not more than 20 hugging the earth. She was trying to hide herself.

Bhim looked at her and said," do not worry. I am not like the others. I will save you, but tell me are you from the Residency?" "Yes"

"Good, there is nothing to worry, were there others with you."

"They were four other ladies, and they were shot but I escaped from a window and have travelled a few miles and have been hiding here till I couldn't control my cough and you heard it and now I'm at your mercy."

He looked at the girl and said, "no you're not at my mercy, but at the mercy of the Lord Krishna, I will save you but come because if the other soldiers see you, they will kill you or they will try to do something worse with you."

the-river-of-no-return-a-
love-story

As the girl got up Bhim was struck by her beauty. She was pure English, extremely fair, and her dress accentuated a voluptuous body. She realized her predicament and attempted to cover herself with her hands, but Bhima took his cloak with the ensign of the Bengal regiment and gave it to her. " Wear it," he said," you will feel more confident."

The girl wore the cloak. Bhima could now observe her face closely and realized that she was naturally beautiful, but, she appeared more like the Goddess Rukmani.

Suddenly he heard voices, shouting," Bhim Singh where are you?"

Bhim held his finger to his lips and whispered, "Come with me."

As she caught Bhim's hand, she felt reassured. Bhim cocked his rifle and slid the cartridge into the sleeve. He told the girl, "Just lie behind these trees and let me find out who these men are."

He shouted, "Who are you"

Somebody asked," Are you, Bhim?"

"Yes, I'm coming."

Bhim came out of the thicket and saw two soldiers from his regiment. They were with rifles. One of them asked, "Have you seen the English girl? I am told she ran away from the residency."

"I have not seen anybody"

One of the soldiers was a little suspicious. "I don't think he's telling the truth," he commented.

The other soldier said," You better tell us the truth because you've been missing from the camp for quite some time after the morning roll call."

The girl coughed again. She probably couldn't control the irritation in her throat, but the unmistakable sound reached the two soldiers and they looked at Bhim and said, "Bastard. The girl is here, and you are lying to us now hand her over to us."

Bhim now did something he had not planned to do. He was already pointing his rifle at one of the soldiers, and he just pulled the trigger. A shot rang out, and the bullet hit the soldier and he crumbled down. The other soldiers shouted, " What have you done, you have killed your brother, for a Firangi."

He knew that there was no going back. He again fired and the second soldier was also taken unaware and he crumpled on the earth. Bhim came back to the girl who clung to him. She felt assured that nothing would happen to her as Bhim had killed two soldiers.

"You could have handed me to them and saved yourself"

"No," he replied, "I do not believe in such things. I remember that a Firangi saved my life when he could have run away during the battle in Waziristan and I have to repay the debt." The girl looked at Bhim apprehensively and asked, "What are we going to do now?"

"We will cross the Ganga. There are loyal troops of my regiment there and you will be safe."

"How will we reach the Ganga; your colleagues will soon find out that two of their brothers are dead."

Bhim smiled. He was handsome, strong, and muscular and said softly, "I have not worn bangles, and do not worry my dear, I'm going to save you. Come with me." The girl got up but it was apparent to Bhim that she was limping and he asked," What has happened."

" I think I twisted my ankle, I can't walk."

Bhim didn't utter a word and just cradled the girl in his arms, and as he cradled her, he felt a tremendous thrill. Her soft body like a rose petal seemed to permeate him, and he felt he was carrying a goddess.

"Don't worry, my princess," he said

"I am not a princess"

"No? yes, but for me, you are a princess and I will save you. Just keep quiet."

"How will you save me?"

"There is a raft which is moored some distance away. It belongs to a friend of mine who has gone to his village. We will go there and cross the Ganga."

"Rowing across the Ganga is so dangerous. It's full of crocodiles"

"Yes it is, there is danger but we will face it as the Lord is on our side."

Bhim grasped the girl close to his chest, and slowly began to walk taking the cover of the trees towards the banks of the Ganga. His heartbeat quickened and the blood rushed to his brain because he could hear the voice of the Subedar Major. The words cut him like a knife as the Subedar was shouting, "Bring the canon forward and aim at the raft which he will try to reach and blow Bhim and the girl to hell."

Bheema hugged the girl more closely to his chest and quickened his gait. He was a fine specimen of a human being as he headed for the raft. He had walked a little distance, and the girl could see the raft moored at the river bank. Out of the corner of her eye far away, she saw the sepoys pushing the canon forward. She was frightened and closed her eyes.

"We are reaching," Bhim whispered.

They were nearing the raft and suddenly they could hear loud voices and he could hear the Subedar Major shouting," Bhim Singh has killed two of my men and taken the girl. Fire the cannon and sink the raft. But before you kill them capture the girl so we can teach her a lesson she will never forget."

The hustle and bustle was all around and the cannon spat fire. The first salvo missed the raft and very soon Bhim had reached and quickly jumped on the raft with the girl s cradled in his arms and gently lowered her on the wooden deck. He began to push the raft away from the edge of the river with the available oar on the raft

There was all-around firing. As the raft moved into the river, Bhim cocked his rifle and fired twice in quick succession. The cannon roared again but Bhim and the girl were further away and the shot fell in the water. He was a good shot and his aim was lethal. He had found his target and saw two men fall far away.

The raft was heading into the open river, dark clouds were hovering in the sky and he knew it would rain. Maybe there could be a thunderstorm. He must escape with the girl quickly across the Ganga before the soldiers catch up with him. The other soldiers now fired, but they were firing recklessly and the aim was not there. The girl hugged the raft, which was now moving slowly forward to the river centre. The shots had ceased as they moved across the Ganga.

The girl looked at him and said, " I don't know how to thank you."

"You don't have to thank me. I have done what Lord Krishna would have done."

"You are a very brave man"

The heavens opened up and rain began to fall on the river. In such a murky atmosphere the crocodiles seem to have gone under the water, and Bhim whispered " Do not worry we shall soon cross the river. "They were now in the deep portion of the mighty river and then far away they could see two crocodiles moving towards them. With the rain falling, the visibility was low, but the girl could see the two crocodiles." Can you see them?" She asked.

"Yes, I've seen them"

"Will they attack us?"

"They probably will until I shoot one of them, and then, perhaps seeing the blood of their brethren, they may not come forward"

Bhim fired and hit one of the crocodiles in the eye. It was a terrible thing to do and soon the water was turning red with the blood of the crocodile. But now the other crocodiles had stopped and soon he was across the river to the other side. It was still raining as he carried the girl gently from the raft and laid her under a tree. The dress clung to her body and Bhim was witness to all her charms. For him, she was a goddess. He could make out her breasts and also her beautiful thighs. The rain increased in frenzy and involuntarily Bhim held the girl close to him. Her aroma intoxicated him and the girl also had a strange desire. A desire to reward this man, whose name she didn't know.

The end or the beginning

The moment is created by god. With the thunderstorm on Bhim spontaneously kissed the girl. He was apprehensive but the girl's heart was thumping like mad and the words formed in her mouth,' Yes, yes I will Yes.' But it all ended in a groan as Bhim had laid her and with the rain beating on his back took her swiftly like an animal in heat in the rain. After it was over he whispered, " We are now safe. we are just about 3 to 4 miles away from the Cantonment where loyal troops are available. I will take you there."

She looked at him and said," You are a handsome man, and you have done a lot for me".

Spontaneously the girl bent forward and kissed him on the lips. "I don't know, but if you wish, I wouldn't mind spending my life with you."

"No, my lady, this cannot happen the sun and the moon cannot meet"

With these words, lifted her and walked towards Cantonment. As they neared there was a shout, " Stop, I will shoot you how come you're carrying an English girl with you?"

The girl shouted," he has saved me, please don't fire." some of the soldiers now came out along with the captain of the East India Company Army. They came and the captain told Bhima you have risked your life for this, I will reward you."

"I don't need anything, sir, I have already got the reward."

The girl was taken away and she looked back but probably that was the last time she saw him. Bhim vanished in the rain but later in England, the girl realised she was with child. Well friend what happened next is another story .

Cotton Green is one of the suburbs of the city of Bombay now known as Mumbai. For this tale, I will use the term Bombay because it gives a nostalgic feeling of the British Raj and the way the city mushroomed to what it is now. Cotton Green holds the Cotton exchange. The Cotton Exchange is like the stock exchange and raw cotton, which is grown in the hinterland of western India is traded here. This area also abuts the Bombay docks and all the land is owned by the Bombay Port Trust. They have massive storage sheds here and goods worth millions of dollars are stored till disposed all over the country. At one time, Bombay was the premier port of India.

But in this vast melee of sheds and docks, a small portion has been leased by the BPT to the Indian Air Force. This forms the Air Force station. Cotton Green is a beautiful place in a commercial jungle and in those days, it was the headquarters of the Bombay Air Force. My commander was Wing Commander PN Mehra, who sadly is no more. I was posted as a youngster at the station headquarters and was appointed Adjutant to PN Mehra. The Air Force station also houses the officers mess a quaint structure that had been built before the start of the Second World War. During the war, Italian POW's were housed in cotton green and the man in charge was a Sergeant Major of the British army. They was one small cottage now called the VIP cottage, which was the residence of the Sergeant Major. I am told the Italian POW were pretty happy to stay in Cotton Green, and they lived a reasonable life free from the tensions of Europe, where the battle was on between the Axis powers and the Allies.

This story commences when I sat down in my chair as the adjutant of the Air Force station, I had my first meeting with the station commander, and we both got along very well. I came out of his room and had a look at my office. My office had a veranda with a barbed wire fencing abutting a small road. I was standing in the veranda when I observed a beautiful girl with a satchel walking briskly on the road behind the Barbwire.

The moment I saw the girls I liked her immensely. She was slim of medium height and wore a frock about 2 inches above the knee displaying a set of beautiful legs. She was fair and I could make out that she must be of Portuguese decent.

She saw me standing on the veranda, but didn't say anything and walked away. Now it became routine for me to stand close to the fence and watch the girl walk past me. I would watch her coming towards me from a distance and moment she reached the place where she was in my eye, I would find that she has slowed down and once she stopped and just looked at me. She probably could have made out that I was an officer of the Indian Air Force and this state of affairs continued for close to a month.

Once sitting at the bar with my friend, Joginder, who was the engineering officer of the helicopter unit, I told him about the girl walking past the barbed wire fence. He replied. "Why didn't you tell me earlier? I could have helped."

"I was thinking about it," I replied.

"Okay", he said ,"if you like he so much, I will help."

"Yes," I replied, "I'm just wondering how do I get an intro to her?"

"Why don't you just yell to her when she is crossing the wire and say hello?"

I said," you can't be serious. I am an officer and there are many men all around. It will look very bad and maybe the girl may not like it."

"Okay," Joginder replied," I will do something for you. I will find out who she is, and what is going to happen."

A few days lapsed, and I still continued standing in the veranda watching the girl. To me she looked extremely beautiful. I could make out. She was not Local Maharashtra girl, and obviously she had European blood in her. Maybe I thought she must be from Goa, which was earlier, a Portuguese Colony..

A few days later, Joginder again met me in the bar and we clinked glasses with Black Knight whiskey, which was a popular brand in those days. I don't see this brand now. Probably the manufacturers have either discontinued it.

"What information you have, my friend," I asked.

"Well," he replied, "her name is Rosie Ferrao and she is of Portuguese origin and one of her grandparents was a Portuguese who is now in Portugal and even her father and mother are planning to go there.

"What about her?" I asked.

"Well, she's a clerk in the Bombay Port trust office and attends the law course at the KC college, evening classes."

"Why is that?"

"I don't know. Maybe she is a studious type as well. What are you going to do?"

I thought for a moment and said ,"we both are going to join college to study law."

"You have use the word, we"

"Yes," I said," you're going to give me company. Are you not?"

He clapped his hands and said," yes, we are friends and we will both enrolled in the KC college for the evening law course of Bombay University."

I made my application to join the evening course to PN Mera and he duly approved it, and both of us enrolled as law students in the KC college.

On the very first day of the evening class, just before the professor came, I walked up to Rosy. She was a little surprised to see me because she had seen me standing in the veranda of the station headquarters. I did not waste any time. I just walked up to her and said I have also joined the course. I introduced myself and both of us sat down on the same desk. That was the beginning, and it's soon transformed, into a close kinship. Frankly, I was not interested in doing the law course, but I didn't want to fail either, so I put in my best efforts to attend the course. Joginder also joined in, and he became friends with a Maratha girl who always accompanied Rosie.

The classes used to be over at 8 PM and I used to come and go on my royal Enfield motorbike. This was the one given to me by my father. One day when we were coming out of the classes, I suggested to Rosie to come for a ride on my motorbike, Joginder had a scooter and he took Rosie's friend away, and this girl was left with me. She sat at the back of my motorbike and the machine became alive and like a panther it speeded through Bombay.

I drove to Nariman point, which in those days was a pretty desolate place at about nine in the evening, and then from Nariman point, I drove along Marine Drive up to Malabar Hill down to Haji Ali where we stopped and had ice cream. It was an accelerating drive and at the end of it when we were eating ice cream, she confessed that it was the first time she had set on the motorbike, and it was so wonderful..

Now it became a daily occurrence between us that after classes, we would drive out together and many a time we drove up to the hilltop restaurant on Malabar Hill, sat there, and I shared a glass of beer. After a few such meetings our intimacy increased and we both liked each other.

One day we were sitting in the restaurant and the Malabar Hill overlooking the Bombay city. When the monsoon broke, the monsoon is the most beautiful time in Bombay and the weather becomes cool..

The restaurant was almost empty because of the heavy rain and I suggested that it would take some time before we could leave this place. I asked her where are you staying and she told me that she was staying at a girls hostel.

"Fine," I said," I'll drop you there, but let the rain finish."

The downpour, however, became more torrential, and after that time, and for the first time, I held her hands and gently squeeze them. She did not withdraw her hands and we both kept holding them while sitting and watching the rain as it beat on the earth. The Bombay city was clouded with the rain and we could just see some of the lights of this glorious city.. Instinctively I got up and lifted her from the chair. They were nobody there except another couple. I walked out into the adjacent Kamla Nehru Garden. Rain beat on both of us and she asked me what the hell are you doing?

"Nothing," I replied, "holding you in my arms, so I can protect you from the rain."

"Isn't it silly? We were pretty safe in the restaurant, and now you have come out here in the garden and it's raining heavily."

"Yes, it's right. It is silly, but that is because of you and honestly I must tell you that I like you very much."

With the rain falling, I applied my lips to her and kissed her. This soon turned into a last vicious kiss, and our mouth is opened, and the rain water went into our mouth along with the tongue. I later on a bench and with the rain falling over and pulled up her T-shirt and bra, and was witnessed to set up beautiful breasts. I began to suck her nipples while Rosie kept eyes shut as the rain had now become torrential downpour. At the back of my mind, I knew this was a magical moment, something that would never happen again. The Bombay monsoon is something wonderful. It can rain for a long time and plants flood the city and this was going through the days. There were nobody in the garden took me and my girl in the rain visibility was zero, and we could not even see the restaurant from where we were, covered the entire PARK. She had a skirt on, and I put my hands under a hand began to it panty. I am a strong man and the frizzy lingerie, not used to search the ferocious assault at the seam. I pulled it off and pocket it to keep it as a souvenir. There is nothing more to add as Lord Krishna, probably himself came down to the union with the thunder, rain and lightning fletching across the sky. It is a moment which I will never forget all my life..

After it was over, we leave painting and rain continued, but I covered her completely, and just kept kissing her.

Much later, I dropped her at the hostel and been back into the office mess.

This state affairs continued for a month and we were both insatiable. We travels Bombay up and down to Juhu beach and Bandra, and at every moment, the end result was victory for both of us. The monsoon has its part to play in this, and I just can't forget that once with the rain and lightning thundering, I had held and coconut tree on the Juhu beach and the inevitable happened.

My heart was thumping loudly and I looked at Rosie.. I was wondering what's going to happen. Unknown to me, my antiques were known to the station commander as the Air Force pro unit for keeping your watch.

My misdemeanour was reported to the station command who called me and said "look young man. I know what has happened. You have a girlfriend but this relationship is not in your interest, and as you are not even 25 and cannot get married. I am recommending that you be moved immediately hostage to the east.

He looked at his watch, and with penalty said," the EN 12 is waiting and you just take your bag and move out. You will think for me. You will thank me for this later on."

That was it. I was moved almost 2000 miles away to Bagdogra. I did not even have time to say goodbye to Rosie. I tried her telephone a couple of times and the BPT office, but she didn't pick it up, and after a couple of months, I came back to Bombay, I registered myself for the law course and went there, and I asked the professor about Rosie. He told me she had left and gone away without completing her course.

I searched all over for her, but I never had her Goa address. Many months later I did get hold of it and went there and met the caretaker of the house. He shook my hands and said," I don't know what you're talking, but the girl has left a few months back with her father and mother for Portugal, and we have no forwarding address, anyway, what's your relationship with her?"

I didn't say anything, but just kept silent, and after sometime, I said," it's nothing. It's not important."

My heart was thumping wildly again, but this time it was like I had been defeated. The Lord had promised me something and then snatched it away. What did it mean? I have never been able to understand the mysteries of Lord, but this incident is my in my mind, and I thought I could share it with my readers as a true story, of love.

CHAPTER NINETEEN

A STRANGE TALE

I'm going to narrate a very strange tale, and do not know whether it was a mystic experience or a reality or a figment of my imagination. I had had been asked to move from Bagdogra to Jammu and put in charge of a fighter squadron. War clouds were hovering and my squadron was slated to go into battle.

Jammu is very close to the temple to the Goddess Durga. I decided to pay a visit there before entering combat and accordingly took my SUV and began the drive. I wanted to pay my respects and come back quickly because in the morning I was supposed to take off in a sortie to scour the enemy in the Hills.

I drove slowly through the hills, and then I stopped because on the left side stood a beautiful girl with a small bag. I was little surprised seeing her and asked her how come she was standing here like this

"Sir," the girl replied ,"I was travelling by bus, but the bus had a flat tyre and we all got down and I had just gone to the bushes to relieve myself and when I returned I found the bus had left without me."

I scratched my head and wondered whether she was telling the truth because generally the drivers take all passengers with them. But still when I saw the girl and her mesmerising beauty, I hoped she could be telling the truth. She had her sari tied below the navel of her belly, and looked lovely.

"Okay," I said," get in the front seat; where do you want to go?"

She looked at me and said I would like to go to the temple of the Goddess Durga, but before that can we just drive along this road to a small temple.

"Okay ," I replied, "no harm in that."

I put my car into gear and we began to move up the hill. It's a pretty steep hill and the engine was puffing away in second gear. Soon the temple came to sight and she said "stop."

I stopped the vehicle and she got down and went inside the temple. I kept sitting in my SUV, waiting for her.

A good 15 minutes passed, and the girl didn't come out of the temple and I was wondering what's happened. I decided to check and got down from SUV and went inside the temple. It was a small temple but I was in front of bloody shock because inside the temple, there was nobody. I wondered where the girl had vanished . I noticed a small door at the back and I thought she might have gone out of the door but I was wondering why she went out of the door and why she didn't come back to the SUV ?

I wanted to shout for her, but then I realise that I didn't even know her name so I shouted ,"girl, girl where are you?."

My voice echoed in the hills and could be heard miles away but then was wondering what happened and I want to go back to my SUV. I thought the girl had run away but somehow my mind was not convinced and I was wondering that something strange is going to happen, for the simple reason the girl was so beautiful and I admit it fuelled my imagination.

I sat before the deity which was of Lord Shiva closed my eyes and began to pray. I thought I would pay my obeisance and then continue to the temple.

I got up and was planning to leave when I heard rustle and I was absolutely taken back to see the girl enter inside through the door. Well I thought that solves the mystery. She had gone out of the door to her village and come back.. But I had nagging doubts because the girl had an beauty about her and it was not something which a village girl would have. But what surprised me more, the girl entered before me now was attired in a different dress. She had the exotic saree and a blouse just got so low there is nothing much to hide..

She had wonderful eyes and a smooth complexion and somehow I couldn't accept the fact that this girl could be from the village. I would more likely relate her to a high class family because she looked more like a princess.

The girl came to me and put her hands on my shoulder and said ,"Capt. God has decided to give you a gift."

"What gift?"

"You will find out soon enough."

"But what about this gift?"

The girls smiles and says, "you are a warrior a Kshatriya and tomorrow you are going to battle and today the gods are going to give you something which you will cherish and a person will come in your life. I will give you a ring and that will bring you good luck in the battle tomorrow, otherwise the gods have noted great danger to you."

I was not impressed and I asked ,"why should God be impressed with me I am still a bachelor and living my life happily."

"Yes," she said, "you are a man of God a man of principle and in the true sense like Arjuna a great warrior. The gods have seen your life and seen that many times you spared the enemy so that he could survive. You are a man of chivalry and I am pretty sure you deserve what you're going to get."

"OK," I said, "but where is the gift?"

She bent forward, and kissed my eyes and whisper softly," I am the gift."

As it happens, there were a crash of thunder and it began to rain heavily outside and here I was with this beautiful girl in the small temple of Shiva. I looked out of the door and see that the rain is beating on the earth and the visibility reduced. I could see that my SUV, but become invisible because of the thick fog which is coming up, the girl kept looking at me and then she gently kissed me on my lips.

I thought this girl is just cooking up a tail about the gods and the gift. I thought she's a lonely girl and maybe she's looking for an outlet for her energy. But t the more I saw her, the more I realized that beauty was ethereal, her eyes, deep and blue, perfectly warm lips and aquiline nose, slender neck and then her bust so beautiful that one wonder what they would look if they were free.

After a moment the girl kissed me once more and ran out of the back door to the rain

"Look," I said ,"don't go into the rain. It can be trouble. You could get a chill."

Outside the rain is beating heavily of the earth and when I looked out of the door, I couldn't make out the girl and then I saw her just a few feet away and she was absolutely drenched and this only added to her sexiness.

I shouted above the noise of the thunder and the rain, "Immediately come inside,"

She just looked and didn't answer.

"Okay," I said ,"I'm coming"

I was concerned for the girl in the rain and stepped out and soon reached her, and gathered her in my arms and began to walk back to the safety of the temple.

She sneezed and that was cause for concern. I was wondering what to say when she did something which took my breath away. "I am wet" she said ,"and I don't want to get a chill" She followed up by opening the buttons of her blouse and took it off. She was not wearing a bra and her breast's beauty captivated me.

She softly whispered, "Come , just touch me," I couldn't wait any longer and slowly brought my hand and touched her breast. I touched her breast like she was a porcelain doll. "touch me," she whispered. I was emboldened and I unravelled her sari. It fell in a heap at her feet. I gently lifted her and placed her on the floor, parted her thighs to witness her esoteric delight. I spread the folds and buried my face and sought her innermost recess. Outside the rain continued and now there was thunder and lightning. She paid her tribute and now I felt like a tiger I closed my eyes and was bewildered, I saw myself flying and following me was the enemy fighter,

Oh god what's happening.!

The taste of her, the smell of her, the feel of her so close to me , skin to skin, time and space had no meaning anymore. There was only her." I closed my eyes and again saw the enemy fighter. He was behind me and he fired his guns. The salvo almost hit me and now I think, I'm going to lose, What's happening? I opened my eyes and realised I was on top of the beauty. I thrust into her.

As I close my eyes, I see myself in the plane and realize I'm lucky there was not much damage and I decided the time had come to do the cobra Manoeuvre. I put my plane in a 90° vertical climb, which surprised the enemy, and I was behind him and fired my guns, I hit his plane and I could see the pilot eject from the plane. I didn't want to hurt him, and I flew back to base.

As I landed the ground crew , rush and help me out and say ," Sir, you put in a great fight". I am bewildered because I remember that I was in the temple making love to the most beautiful woman in the world. Was it all a dream, fantasy? I cannot tell as the air crew van took me to, the base operations room.

CHAPTER TWENTY

ROSY FERRAO

Cotton Green is one of the suburbs of the city of Bombay now known as Mumbai. For this tale, I will use the term Bombay because it gives a nostalgic feeling of the British Raj and the way the city mushroomed to what it is now. Cotton Green holds the Cotton exchange. The Cotton Exchange is like the stock exchange and raw cotton, which is grown in the hinterland of western India is traded here. This area also abuts the Bombay docks and all the land is owned by the Bombay Port Trust. They have massive storage sheds here and goods worth millions of dollars are stored till disposed all over the country. At one time, Bombay was the premier port of India.

But in this vast melee of sheds and docks, a small portion has been leased by the BPT to the Indian Air Force. This forms the Air Force station. Cotton Green is a beautiful place in a commercial jungle and in those days, it was the headquarters of the Bombay Air Force. My commander was Wing Commander PN Mehra, who sadly is no more. I was posted as a youngster at the station headquarters and was appointed Adjutant to PN Mehra. The Air Force station also houses the officer's mess a quaint structure that had been built before the start of the Second World War. During the war, Italian POWs were housed in cotton green and the man in charge was a Sergeant Major of the British army. There was one small cottage now called the VIP cottage, which was the residence of the Sergeant Major. I am told the Italian POWs were pretty happy to stay in Cotton Green, and they lived a reasonable life free from the tensions of Europe, where the battle was on between the Axis powers and the Allies.

This story commences when I sat down in my chair as the adjutant of the Air Force station, I had my first meeting with the station commander, and we both got along very well. I came out of his room and had a look at my office. My office had a veranda with barbed wire fencing abutting a small road. I was standing on the veranda when I observed a beautiful girl with a satchel walking briskly on the road behind the Barbwire.

The moment I saw the girls I liked her immensely. She was slim of medium height and wore a frock about 2 inches above the knee displaying a set of beautiful legs. She was fair and I could make out that she must be of Portuguese descent.

She saw me standing on the veranda but didn't say anything and walked away. Now it became routine for me to stand close to the fence and watch the girl walk past me. I would watch her coming towards me from a distance and the moment she reached the place where she was in my eye, I would find that she has slowed down and once she stopped and just looked at me. She probably could have made out that I was an officer of the Indian Air Force and this state of affairs continued for close to a month.

Once sitting at the bar with my friend, Joginder, who was the engineering officer of the helicopter unit, I told him about the girl walking past the barbed wire fence. He replied. "Why didn't you tell me earlier? I could have helped."

"I was thinking about it," I replied.

"Okay", he said," if you like him so much, I will help."

"Yes," I replied, "I'm just wondering how do I get an intro to her?"

"Why don't you just yell to her when she is crossing the wire and say hello?"

I said," You can't be serious. I am an officer and there are many men all around. It will look very bad and maybe the girl may not like it."

"Okay," Joginder replied," I will do something for you. I will find out who she is, and what is going to happen."

A few days lapsed, and I still continued standing in the veranda watching the girl. To me, she looked extremely beautiful. I could make out. She was not a local Maharashtra girl, and obviously, she had European blood in her. Maybe I thought she must be from Goa, which was earlier, a Portuguese Colony..

A few days later, Joginder again met me in the bar and we clinked glasses with Black Knight whiskey, which was a popular brand in those days. I don't see this brand now. Probably the manufacturers have discontinued it.

"What information do you have, my friend," I asked.

"Well," he replied, "her name is Rosie Ferrao and she is of Portuguese origin one of her grandparents was a Portuguese who is now in Portugal and even her father and mother are planning to go there.

"What about her?" I asked.

"Well, she's a clerk in the Bombay Port Trust office and attends the law course at the KC college, evening classes."

"Why is that?"

"I don't know. Maybe she is a studious type as well. What are you going to do?"

I thought for a moment and said," We both are going to join college to study law."

"You have to use the word, we"

"Yes," I said," you're going to give me company. Are you not?"

He clapped his hands and said," Yes, we are friends and we will both be enrolled in the KC College for the evening law course at Bombay University."

I made my application to join the evening course to PN Mera and he duly approved it, and both of us enrolled as law students in the KC college.

On the very first day of the evening class, just before the professor came, I walked up to Rosy. She was a little surprised to see me because she had seen me standing in the veranda of the station headquarters. I did not waste any time. I just walked up to her and said I have also joined the course. I introduced myself and both of us sat down on the same desk. That was the beginning, and it's soon transformed, into a close kinship. Frankly, I was not interested in doing the law course, but I didn't want to fail either, so I put in my best efforts to attend the course. Joginder also joined in, and he became friends with a Maratha girl who always accompanied Rosie.

The classes used to be over at 8 PM and I used to come and go on my Royal Enfield motorbike. This was the one given to me by my father. One day when we were coming out of the classes, I suggested to Rosie to come for a ride on my motorbike, Joginder had a scooter and he took Rosie's friend away, and this girl was left with me. She sat at the back of my motorbike and the machine became alive and like a panther it speeded through Bombay.

I drove to Nariman Point, which in those days was a pretty desolate place at about nine in the evening, and then from Nariman Point, I drove along Marine Drive up to Malabar Hill down to Haji Ali where we stopped and had ice cream. It was an accelerating drive and at the end of it when we were eating ice cream, she confessed that it was the first time she had set on the motorbike, and it was so wonderful..

Now it became a daily occurrence between us that after classes, we would drive out together and many a time we drove up to the hilltop restaurant on Malabar Hill, sat there, and I shared a glass of beer. After a few such meetings our intimacy increased and we both liked each other.

One day we were sitting in the restaurant and Malabar Hill overlooking Bombay City. When the monsoon broke, the monsoon is the most beautiful time in Bombay and the weather becomes cool..

The restaurant was almost empty because of the heavy rain and I suggested that it would take some time before we could leave this place. I asked her where she was staying and she told me that she was staying at a girls hostel.

"Fine," I said," I'll drop you there, but let the rain finish."

The downpour, however, became more torrential, and after that time, and for the first time, I held her hands and gently squeeze them. She did not withdraw her hands and we both kept holding them while sitting and watching the rain as it beat on the earth. The Bombay city was clouded with the rain and we could just see some of the lights of this glorious city.. Instinctively I got up and lifted her from the chair. They were nobody there except another couple. I walked out into the adjacent Kamla Nehru Garden. Rain beat on both of us and she asked me what the hell are you doing?

"Nothing," I replied, "holding you in my arms, so I can protect you from the rain."

"Isn't it silly? We were pretty safe in the restaurant, and now you have come out here in the garden and it's raining heavily."

"Yes, it's right. It is silly, but that is because of you and honestly I must tell you that I like you very much."

With the rain falling, I applied my lips to her and kissed her. This soon turned into a last vicious kiss, and our mouth is opened, and the rain water went into our mouth along with the tongue. I later on a bench and with the rain falling over over and pulled up her T-shirt and bra, and was witnessed to set up beautiful breasts. I began to suck her nipples while Rosie kept eyes shut as the rain had now become torrential downpour. At the back of my mind, I knew this was a magical moment, something that would never happen again. The Bombay monsoon is something wonderful. It can rain for a long time and plants flood the city and this was going through the days. There were nobody in the garden took me and my girl in the rain visibility was zero, and we could not even see the restaurant from where we were, covered the entire PARK. She had a skirt on, and I put my hands under a hand began to it panty. I am a strong man and the frizzy lingerie, not used to search the ferocious assault at the seam. I pulled it off and pocket it to keep it as a souviner. There is nothing more to add as Lord Krishna, probably himself came down to the union with the thunder, rain and lightning fletching across the sky. It is a moment which I will never forget all my life..

After it was over, we leave painting and rain continued, but I covered her completely, and just kept kissing her.

Much later, I dropped her at the hostel and been back into the office mess.

This state affairs continued for a month and we were both insatiable. We travels Bombay up and down to Juhu beach and Bandra, and at every moment, the end result was victory for both of us. The monsoon has its part to play in this, and I just can't forget that once with the rain and lightning thundering, I had held and coconut tree on the Juhu beach and the inevitable happened.

My heart was thumping loudly and I looked at Rosie.. I was wondering what's going to happen. Unknown to me, my antiques were known to the station commander as the Air Force pro unit for keeping your watch.

My misdemeanour was reported to the the station command who called me and said "look young man. I know what has happened. You have a girlfriend but this relationship is not in your interest, and as you are not even 25 and cannot get married. I am recommending that you be moved immediately hostage to the east.

He looked at his watch, and with penalty said," the EN 12 is waiting and you just take your bag and move out. You will think for me. You will thank me for this later on."

That was it. I was moved almost 2000 miles away to Bagdogra. I did not even have time to say goodbye to Rosie. I tried her telephone a couple of times and the BPT office, but she didn't pick it up, and after a couple of months, I came back to Bombay, I registered myself for the law course and went there, and I asked the professor about Rosie. He told me she had left and gone away without completing her course.

I searched all over for her, but I never had her Goa address. Many months later I did get hold of it and went there and met the caretaker of the house. He shook my hands and said," I don't know what you're talking, but the girl has left a few months back with her father and mother for Portugal, and we have no forwarding addres, anyway, what's your relationship with her?"

I didn't say anything, but just kept silent, and after sometime, I said," it's nothing. It's not important."

My heart was thumping wildly again, but this time it was like I had been defeated. The Lord had promised me something and then snatched it away. What did it mean? I have never been able to understand the mysteries of Lord, but this incident is my in my mind, and I thought I could share it with my readers as a true story, of love.